# DARK ILLUSION

## THE ARONDIGHT CODEX - BOOK TWO

### NICOLE R. TAYLOR

# PROLOGUE

The air was full of the scents of rebirth. Blood, ash, brimstone, and Darkness.

He dragged the needle through his flesh, his teeth grinding to keep his pain contained. His legion of Infernals swirled around him, aiding him with their essence. It was laborious work—the delicate operation taking many days and weeks to complete.

He couldn't take over a living creature the way his soldiers could. Those bodies deteriorated over time—they were weak and couldn't wield Darkness. A demon of his power required something a little more...*durable*. So he was forced to stitch together the strongest pieces of fresh corpses, weaving Darkness into the flesh and bone, turning the congealed blood black.

As one of the greater races of his species, he could take on a human appearance through his shell, but his demonic essence always bled through. Teeth, eyes, and claws were his bane, though Darkness helped hide his true nature from the human world. Glamours would come later, once his body was fully formed.

The Light called him a Balan, a king of Hell that commanded legions of demons, full of cunning and the ruthless desire for sin, but after his failure at the Naturals' London Sanctum, he was king of *nothing*.

He gasped as his fingers slid through his damp hair. He was red and sticky, his new face unfamiliar and raw.

A wall of fire erupted into life around him, circling his shell, raining down searing heat onto his raw flesh. He dropped to his knees, his needle falling to the carpet only to be lost amongst the fibres.

"My Lord," he said, feeling the presence of his father, the one from who they all came.

"*Markzoth.*"

Names had power amongst their kind and how his master knew his, he didn't know. It didn't matter now, he was in his thrall, his Darkness flaring and dying as the sound rumbled around the room.

"I will have Arondight," the demon commanded. "No cost is too great."

Markzoth felt the delicate strings holding his new body together begin to fray under the pressure, but it wasn't his new shell that was being threatened.

"I need time to regain my strength," he said, his teeth elongating through his flimsy glamour.

"The balance is tipping in our favour," the voice declared. "Now is the time to strike."

He bowed his head, his neck stiff. "You will have what you desire, my Lord."

"The girl is the key."

"The plan is already in motion," he replied. "It will be done."

"Another failure will not be tolerated."

The flames flared, then dissipated, leaving behind a black scorch mark on the carpet. Markzoth breathed deeply, the scent of burning synthetic fibre entwined with the heady copper tang of human blood. It smelt like home. The home his kind had before they were forced into this world.

His lord had left him, but as Markzoth resumed the preparations on his new shell, he realised he wasn't alone.

He looked up, his gaze finding a swathe of Darkness hovering before him. *The human boy.*

It was a good day, then. Full of the promise of blood and Darkness. They would come as he knew they would—after all, it was in their nature.

Markzoth smiled and resumed his work, allowing them to see each deliberate stitch through his stinging flesh. They would come, and they would die. It was certain.

All he needed to do was wait.

**1**

---

The library was a ruin around me, the ombré portal swirling like an angry tornado through the shattered remains of the dome.

The scent of phantom smoke filled my nostrils and I scrambled across the floor, my hand curling around the hilt of my arondight blade. As soon as I had it in my grasp, the sword erupted into life, sparking with purple Light.

My throat was raw, and my knees were red with blood, but I pushed to my feet and swung my blade with my last ounce of strength. The demon roared with fury, the sound cutting off with a gurgle as I severed his head from his body.

*I'm waiting for you, Scarlett.*

I jumped as a book slammed down on the table in front of me, bringing my consciousness back to the present. I was in the kitchen at the London Sanctum eating lunch, not battling a greater demon who'd been trying to trick me into selling my soul.

"What's that?" I asked as Wilder slid into the chair opposite. Wilder was my Natural mentor, trainer, and an all-round pain in my arse. "Don't tell me there's bland reading involved."

"You had a lucky break," he said glowering at me, the light catching the subtle silver sheen in his eyes. "There's still a long way to go with your training."

Sighing, I pushed away my half-eaten lunch and dragged the book towards me. The hardcover—simply entitled *Demonology*—was a deep midnight blue with gold embellishments.

"Why didn't anyone think to give me this when I first got here?" I complained as I opened it.

"It's a kids' book," Wilder declared.

*Ugh, he was right.* As I flipped through the pages, I found illustrations of different demons and simplified explanations for each kind of manifestation.

I shot him a pouty look. "Are you trying to tell me something?"

"I'm trying to impart on you the wisdom of a fifteen-year education in as little time as possible," he drawled.

"Is there such a thing as a spell book? Or is it called a Light book?" I wondered. "That could be useful."

"Light doesn't come with an instruction manual," Wilder said with a disgusted look. "It's a personal experience, and different for everyone."

"So how does anyone learn to fully control it if it's unpredictable?"

"I can guide you, but the rest is up to you." He

gave me a pointed look and added, "I don't know why you're so worried. You did just fine in the incursion. I heard you blew off the doors in the gym."

"How do you know that was me?" I demanded. "I was the only one there."

Since the incursion, the Sanctum had been in high-alert. Naturals had been scouring the city for traces of the Balan demon who'd attempted to take over the building and steal the Codex, but so far, no traces had been found. At least we didn't have to worry about the Infernal who'd been trying to alter people's DNA—Wilder had taken it out after he'd excised it from Greer.

"Romy said there was an academy," I said, stroking my fingers over the book. "Where is it?"

"The Cotswolds." *Fancy.*

"Did you go?"

"Yes."

"And?" I prodded.

"And what?"

I rolled my eyes, not interested in prying information from Wilder so early in the day. "What's it like?"

"Like any boarding school that teaches you how to kill demons." He smirked and nodded at the book. "You better study that, Purples. The alert level isn't going to drop until we've found your buddy, the Balan demon."

My scowl deepened. "He's not my buddy. He killed my parents and tried to trick me into selling my soul."

"All the more reason to kick your training into overdrive."

Wilder was so infuriating. He had this thing where he liked to brush off people with his abrasive personality. He was my mentor, and most days he drove me to the brink of fire and brimstone, but I didn't know what I'd do without him. *I so wasn't telling him that.* Talk about complicated.

I was pulled in two directions. Four if I took my heart into account. North and south were the Human Convergence Project and the search for Arondight. East and west were Jackson and Wilder. Then they all had their own personal tug of wars, which just made the whole thing confusing as hell.

At the thought of Jackson, I groaned and lowered my head into my hands. My poor best friend, who'd been possessed by a genetically modified Infernal demon, had his DNA mutated, and was now a world champion e-sports bazillionaire. He was also my closest family, had hidden romantic feelings for me, and caught me kissing Wilder—something that would never happen again—in the hall outside my room. To say we'd parted on bad terms was an understatement.

"What now?" Wilder asked with a groan.

"At some point I have to go find Jackson."

He snorted and leaned back in his chair. "Good luck with that, Purples. You might have to flash a little boob to entice him back here."

"*Wilder!*"

"He's the weedy little demon-hybrid that's in unrequited love with you."

"He's also the guy who could help Ramona cure innocent people infected by DNA-altered Infernals," I fired back. "Human Convergence, remember?"

He rolled his eyes. "It's always something with you."

"He was the only person who cared," I murmured, snapping the demonology book closed. "After years of bouncing around foster homes, getting kicked out of school after school, and being the weirdo loner, he was the only one who stuck. And now he hates me."

"That's his problem, not yours."

I snorted, which caused Wilder to take away my unfinished lunch and slide it down the table out of reach. *He could've had the decency to ask if I was finished first.*

"C'mon. You can't do anything about him today. Let's get back to the gym." He rose to his feet and smoothed down his tight black T-shirt. The fabric left nothing to the imagination, and I tried not to stare at his defined muscles. "Don't forget your colouring book."

*Smart-arse.*

I rose to my feet, the bruises on my bruises shrieking at me. What I wouldn't give for a nice hot bath right about now, but *no*, Wilder wanted to humiliate me with more hand-to-hand combat training.

"Hey, there you are," Romy said behind us.

I turned, smiling at the Natural who'd fast become a good friend amongst the others who still looked at me with trepidation. Having purple Light wasn't exactly a normal thing around here.

Romy was tall, muscular, yet lithe, and her skin was a flawless ivory—apart from the black geometric tattoos that snaked up and down both arms and onto her neck. She said the designs didn't mean anything, but I wasn't entirely convinced.

"Greer has summoned you to the conservatory," she said, glancing warily at Wilder. Her black hair was in a loose braid today, which was different to her usual severe ponytail.

"We're going to the gym to train," he said, "it'll have to wait."

"She said she'd like to see Scarlett immediately."

Wilder narrowed his eyes, clearly annoyed it was a one-person invite, and I squashed down an irritating pang of jealousy.

"It must be important," I said. "I better go see what she wants. I'll come straight back to the gym, okay, boss?"

He grunted and stalked out of the kitchen, causing a group of younger Naturals to scatter in multiple directions like frightened mice.

"I swear he gets grumpier every time I see him," Romy said making a face. "How do you handle him?"

"He's not so bad," I replied with a shrug. "You just have to get to know him."

She raised her eyebrows.

"Okay, okay," I said, waving her off, "you have to impress him with your slashy-stab-stab sword skills first."

"If you say so." She laughed and nudged me towards the door. "You better not keep Greer waiting."

"Do you know what she wants?" The only time Greer summoned me was when I was in trouble…and I'd gotten into trouble a lot since I arrived. Not even killing the greater demon who'd tried to steal the Codex had lifted my probation.

"Like she'd tell me," Romy said with a huff. "Maybe you'll get lucky and they'll let you leave the Sanctum now."

"Cool. I was itching for a visit to Primark for some new pants."

She laughed and shooed me away. "Always a pleasure, Scarlett."

---

The London Sanctum was a hive of activity as I walked down the corridors.

It was a far cry from the first time I'd been here. The Naturals weren't as prolific at procreation as they used to be, so their numbers were quite low. Even with the other Sanctums around the world, there weren't enough of us left to protect humanity completely against the demons. I guess that's what made my purpleness so interesting.

Arondight, AKA the Indigo Flame… Supposedly, I'd come into contact with the mystical blade revered by the Naturals as a child, but I didn't remember. That suspected contact was what made my Light so special. It was tinged with the violet hue of the weapon both sides of the war coveted beyond all else.

I had recollections of the night my parents died and the demon who'd murdered them—the same demon who'd lead the attack on the Sanctum—but that's all I knew. I hadn't even known I was a Natural until that fateful meeting with Wilder outside the pub I used to work at in Camden Town.

So, apparently, I was the last person—besides my parents—who'd seen Arondight in a thousand years. Trouble was, I didn't have any clue where it was, even though the Codex had shown me a vision.

*Stupid Scarlett, touching things she wasn't supposed to, rushing headfirst into danger like a moron.*

The Codex was supposed to burn the unworthy from the inside out, that's why Greer was the only one allowed to touch it. She was the protector, and the head of the London Sanctum, but she was also pure enough to commune with the book and decipher its desires. Technically, I should be a steaming pile of ash, but the Codex had shown me Arondight instead.

The blade still existed, and it was out there some place, waiting to be found.

Passing a group of tradesmen who were reattaching the library doors, I offered them a smile as they stopped and stared at my passing.

As far as they knew, they were repairing some funky storm damage in some obscure academic library, not fixing the remains of a demon incursion. I so couldn't wait until I could learn to use my Light. I'd seen Wilder use his to cloak himself, to make humans forget he was there, and other little bits and pieces, but weaving an illusion on a whole crew of tradesmen was something else entirely.

I clattered up the wrought iron stairs that spiralled up to the conservatory, my footfalls echoing loudly around me. Emerging into the room above, I spotted Greer in the clear glass enclosure that surrounded the pedestal the Codex occupied. Overhead, the dome was full of the grey English sky, giving the whole space a dreary feel.

Greer was wearing her black pantsuit and heels again. Airbrushed and blemish free, everything about her was immaculate as a posed Vogue cover shoot—except this was real life. No wonder Wilder had the hots for her. Sometimes I wondered if I did, too.

"Scarlett," she said as she stepped out of the enclosure with all the grace of an angel, "how is your training progressing?"

"Brutally," I replied, slumping my shoulders.

Greer smiled and stood before me. Reaching out, she grasped my shoulders and straightened me out.

"That's how it's supposed to be," she said, plucking a strand of my purple-tinged hair. It was natural, not dyed at all—supposedly another thing left behind by Arondight.

I corrected my posture and glanced at the Codex. The air shimmered around it, and I could hear the strange siren song it seemed to sing just for me. A low purring sound like a playful kitten you just wanted to pick up and cuddle.

"You wanted to see me about something?" I asked, turning my attention back onto Greer.

Watching me closely, she asked, "Does it still call to you?"

"I keep wanting to look at it," I replied with a frown. "But I figured it does that to everyone."

"No, not everyone." She gestured for me to follow her into the enclosure. "Come. I want to show you something."

Realising she was leading me toward the Codex, I hesitated slightly before I moved with more purpose. I couldn't be afraid of a magic book, even if it had the power to turn me to ash.

The Codex was a record of all the knowledge the Naturals held following the cataclysm that destroyed Camelot almost a thousand years ago. It was the same event that saw Excalibur shatter and Arondight lost, and the Naturals hadn't been the same since. Much of who they—*we*—were was lost. I wasn't the only one whose past was a complete mystery.

It was written in the hand of so many Naturals over hundreds of years, and even those that'd lived to see the mythical Camelot. Not just any old person got to look upon its pages, but to my surprise, Greer closed it before I had the chance.

I stared at the cover, the worn leather nicked and scratched, wondering what this was about. I had a copy tucked underneath my pillow in my room, but this was the real deal.

"Open it," Greer commanded.

Uncertainly flooded through my body. "But…"

"Oh, the cover won't harm you," she said. "It's the pages you have to watch out for."

*Okay then…* I reached out and made to open the Codex, careful not to let my fingers brush the uneven pages underneath. Before I could lift the cover, a zap of energy cracked through my skin and up my arm, flaring an odd shade of violet.

"*Ow!*" I exclaimed, shaking out my hand. "You said it wouldn't do anything!"

"Just as I suspected," Greer said with a smile, clearly pleased I'd just been electrocuted by a *book*. "The Codex is calling out for Arondight."

"What?" I rubbed my temples, which still buzzed with electricity. "You made me touch it, and you didn't know if it'd barbecue me or not?"

"Your contact with the blade protects you," she said. "I always suspected the Light woven into the Codex was something…more. And now I know."

"Something more?"

"It has touches of Arondight's essence, which means the blade wasn't lost at the cataclysm, but much later." She stroked her fingers over the vellum and smiled. "Maybe Arondight wasn't lost, but hidden instead."

"Whatever the sword did to my Light protects me from the Codex's fail-safes?"

"Yes," she stated. "It's quite useful, don't you think?"

I blinked, trying to put the pieces together. I was still new to all this, but the image was sharpening a little each day. "And you think my parents were its guardians and that's why they were killed?"

"Yes, it's a plausible explanation. A veiled order, sworn to protect the Indigo Flame in the ashes of Camelot."

I made a face. A society so secret, not even the Naturals knew it existed? Well, stranger things had happened, I supposed.

"We've rebuilt ourselves since then," I said. "If they've got the sword, why wouldn't they come forward?"

"I don't know. Perhaps they were waiting for something…or someone."

"But my parents died…" I was beginning to believe her crazy theory, which meant my calling hadn't been becoming a Natural, but a guardian in this secret society. That's if, it even existed.

"We don't know for sure, Scarlett," Greer said kindly. "It's all just speculation."

It seemed as if speculation was the word of the year. No one had any concrete answers, just questions layered over more questions, and it was infuriating.

"What do I do?" I asked. "How can I find the trail if I'm not sure there is one to begin with?"

"Continue your training," she replied. "Find your Light and perhaps it will guide you."

"And the Balan?"

"We're still searching and will continue to do so until it's found."

"And Jackson? What about him?"

Greer lowered her gaze, still ashamed over her

past involvement in the Human Convergence Project. It wasn't her fault she'd been deceived, but at least she'd tried to destroy the demon DNA experiments when she'd had the chance.

"We're watching him for now," she said after a pause.

"And?"

"He's safe."

"But I need to go find him," I argued. "Ramona wanted to—"

"I know, Scarlett," Greer interrupted me. "I'm also aware you parted on bad terms, but until Wilder says you're ready to go out into the city, we can't allow you to leave."

I hesitated, curling my hands into tight fists. Wait… Was I stuck in here because they thought I was precious? I wondered when someone was going to tell me that.

"So I was never on probation? This was always about my contact with Arondight?"

"Oh, you're on probation," she corrected me. "Your behaviour has been reckless and slightly arrogant since you've arrived, which makes your training even more important."

"Right…" I made a face and turned away from the Codex. What she meant was, *don't be a smart-arse.*

"Continue your training, Scarlett," Greer said kindly. "Today might not seem like much, but we have new leads to follow. Soon, we may even have a few answers."

*Wouldn't that be a riot?*

I nodded, rubbing my tingling hand against my hip. "And when can I go find Jackson?"

"You'll have to ask Wilder that. I understand he wants you to pass some tests first."

"Tests?" I squeaked. Great… I totally sucked at exams.

"Yes, all of us must pass basic training to be become Naturals, but that's Wilder's area of expertise." She clapped her hands together and smiled brightly. "I've taken up too much of your time already. Good luck, Scarlett."

As I made my way back to the gym, my frown deepened. *Good luck? What was she wishing me luck for?* I guess I was about to find out.

**2**

———

"Purples," Wilder snapped his fingers in front of my face, "you need to listen for this to work."

I nodded, shaking off the uneasiness that'd been following me ever since I'd touched the Codex. The first time, not the second. The image of Arondight locked behind a wall of water had been shadowing my every move, lodged in my dreams, and lately, had begun to encroach on my waking hours, too.

Sometimes I got the feeling we were on a countdown, and in this world of demons and Light versus Dark, that couldn't be good.

"*Scarlett.*"

I tensed and brought my attention back to Wilder. I knew I was in trouble whenever he used my actual name.

We'd taken over a private training room in the gym for the past month, working every day from dawn until dusk. I had to do more than just improve my general fitness and grow my muscles. Training to become a Natural meant I had to fight without thought. Arondight blades and cold iron daggers were just two weapons at my disposal, and there were many more Wilder wanted me to learn. He had me drilling with a staff, spear, axe, and even hand-to-hand— though I hoped I'd never come that close to a demon again. I'd had enough of that ever since that lesser demon tried to lick my eyeball.

Point was, training was gruelling, and I'd only just begun to wake up not feeling like a ball of pain. I supposed that meant I was getting the hang of it.

"Your focus is shot more than usual," Wilder said, narrowing his eyes. "What is it?"

I shrugged. "Nothing."

"Then shall we continue?" He gave me a stern look, then picked up his cold iron dagger from the bench that ran along the wall. "There are several different ways you can excise a demon from a human body, depending on what kind you're dealing with, and how deep its burrowed in its victim."

"You make them sound like a tapeworm," I said, scrunching my nose.

"You can stab it in the heart with a cold iron dagger," he went on, ignoring me. He flipped the blade in his hand and thrust the point into the air to drive home his point. "Another way is to do an exorcism."

"Like you did for Jackson that time?"

"Yeah, like that. If its host is a Vessel, then you've got bigger problems."

"A Vessel? That's people who are willingly possessed, right?"

Wilder nodded. "There's no saving them."

"Why?" I tilted my head to the side. "Surely there's a way?"

"What, by sitting them down with tea and biscuits and giving them good talking to?" He shook his head. "They've sold their souls, Purples. By that point, they've got nothing to go back to."

I pouted and crossed my arms over my chest. "It was still a valid question."

"All this is theory until you can go out into the field," he went on.

"And when will that be?"

"When I say it is."

I shifted my weight from one hip to the other. "How long have you been doing this, exactly?"

"I graduated from the academy when I was seventeen."

On one of my rooftop sulking sessions, he'd told me he was thirty-one, so that meant he'd been hunting demons for fourteen years. It was such a long time to be fighting anything, let alone an incursion of soul-sucking parasites. How did he deal with going out there, knowing there might never be an end to the war?

I didn't know, but it was something I had to come to terms with too, and I wasn't sure I was okay with that.

He stepped to the side, his shoulders tense. "A

possessed human can be unpredictable. Their strength can take you by surprise, so don't let it. Be ready for anything." He began to prowl, circling me on the mat. "The demon needs time to learn how to control each and every new body it jumps, but if threatened, they aren't about to take care of their host. They'll shred their victim to preserve their own life."

"What then? Can it hurt the host?"

Wilder nodded. "We can't let it happen, but it's unavoidable sometimes. Our aim is to stop the demon before it can do any harm. We're here to preserve life."

"Just not demon life."

"Demons are Darkness, and that makes them the mortal enemy of every living thing on Earth." He struck, his fist flying towards me with unnatural speed.

I countered his strike, pushing away his blow with the flat of my forearm. I wasn't fast enough though, and his fist changed trajectory and scraped past my head.

I used the momentum of his body to attack, grabbing his arm and twisting. I pivoted on my heel and I kicked high. My foot slammed into his ribs, but he hardly stumbled.

"Harder!" he shouted. "You kick like a girl!"

Frustration and anger overcame me, and I roared, "*I am a girl!*"

Pushing with all my strength, I slammed my shoulder into his stomach. Wilder barely budged as he grabbed me around the waist and flung me onto the mat. I landed with an *oomph*, then he was on top of me. His hands pinned my arms over my head and I squirmed, my chest heaving.

For a tense moment, he stared at me, his gaze searching mine. Memories of our kiss flooded my mind and it was all I could do not to let them overtake me. He'd initiated it that time, but we haven't spoken about it since. Too much had happened to go back there…and there were too many reasons we couldn't.

Wilder's body was pressing in all the right places and I scowled. "Get off me. You've made your point."

"You let your emotions control you," he murmured, his eyes flashing silver. "When you fight, you need to focus on the movement—where your body is, where your enemy is. When you focus, you can anticipate their next move."

*Boy, I'll say.* I knew exactly where my body was, *and his*. What I couldn't decipher was his next move.

"What about Light?" I asked, my voice taking a husky edge. *Traitor*.

"You can't always rely on Light to save you, Purples. You know what happens when you use too much."

"Yeah, I'll get soul sick and wind up in an irreversible coma," I drawled, remembering the time I'd had to step up and fight an Infernal in the street to save Jackson. The Naturals had left me to my own devices, using me as bait to lure out the demons who'd been genetically altered to infect humans. That's how I'd learned about the after-effects of using too much Light *the hard way*.

Wilder smirked and let me go. "Not much of a picnic, is it?" he asked, pushing to his feet.

"It's like an epic hangover." I rolled my eyes. "I bet you've never been soul sick in your life."

He shrugged, giving away the hint that there was a story there, but knowing how surly and closed-off Wilder could be, I knew I wasn't getting an explanation.

"If you want to find and kill the Balan demon, then you have to suck it up and train harder," he said, holding out his hand. "We got lucky, Purples. His desire to find Arondight blinded him, but he won't make that mistake again."

"I know."

"You take too many unnecessary risks," he continued. "You need to be more calculated with your reactions."

"I know, but I'm trying to learn everything you spent your entire life perfecting. It's not easy."

"Stop making excuses, Purples. It is what it is." He wiggled his hand, becoming irritated I hadn't taken it yet. "A fight is never choreographed. In our world, your opponent wants one thing, and that's killing you."

"Or capture," I argued, sitting up.

"Either way, you're screwed, Purples."

"Don't look so smug."

He sighed. "Take my hand."

Grimacing, I grasped his wrist, and he hauled me up like I weighed nothing at all. He was a tightly wound wall of muscle, after all.

"You're doing okay, Purples," he said, tightening his grip on my wrist. "Time is something we don't have and we're up against it…" I got the feeling he didn't want to pump up my ego too much. Greer was right about that part—I'd made some pretty reckless and arrogant decisions since joining the Naturals.

"We better get back to it then."

His lips quirked and he nodded. "Find your centre, then try again. Don't worry about winning, worry about learning."

Taking a deep breath, I stepped back and pushed away my anger and desire. Then, I struck.

---

*The alley behind 8-bit was dark, the cobblestones damp from the rainstorm that'd just passed over the city.*

*I shivered, sinking deeper into my leather jacket. Uneasiness tugged at me and I glanced towards the street where people were walking back and forth on their way to the pub, or maybe a nightclub or concert. Who knew what people did for fun anymore. I was so far removed from my old life, I'd forgotten how to be human.*

*"You need to go back inside this time," a familiar voice said behind me.*

*I turned, breathing a sigh of relief when I saw a well-known face. "Jackson? I'm sorry it's been so long, but I had to find you. There's…"*

*He turned, his gaze shifting to the mouth of the alley, and pressed his finger to his lips. "Quiet."*

*The feeling that danger wasn't far away crawled up and*

*down my spine, and I reached for my arondight blade. My fingers grazed the hilt, but my best friend shook his head.*

*"That won't work," he said.*

*"What? How—"*

*"Not fast enough," he stated, turning to face the end of the alley.*

*A dark figure melted out of the shadows, edging towards us with a menacing gait. I squinted as its shape phased in and out of being, and while I couldn't keep up with the flickers of black, I felt it. Darkness.*

*Jackson grasped my shoulders and shook, his silver orbs shining brightly in the murky light.*

*Scarlett, wake up.*

I jolted awake and gasped for breath, my feet tangled in my bedsheets. I swiped my forearm across my sticky brow, blinking to shake off the image of my dream.

Above my bed, the stained glass in the skylight was dull, though I could make out the image of the Lady of the Lake. She was a vision of ethereal beauty with her flowing hair and robes, and a sword in her hands. Everyone said it was Arondight, but I liked to think it could also be Excalibur, the blade broken in the cataclysm.

It was a lot to take in at times. The link to the Arthurian legends seemed absurd the first time I heard it, but the more I lived in this world—the world I now belonged to—the more normal it seemed.

Arondight—the Indigo Flame—was never far from my thoughts.

I cursed, realising I was well and truly tangled—in

my sheets and my unknown heritage. Dragging myself out of bed, I shuffled into my little bathroom and washed my face. Lifting my gaze, I stared at my reflection, but I wasn't giving away anything.

How was I supposed to find out about my parents when it was likely they never wanted to be found? And why was I dreaming about Jackson? That shadow had stirred a familiar sensation.

Knowing there was no way in hell I was going back to sleep, I dragged on yesterday's tactical pants and T-shirt, also known as the Naturals totally conspicuous uniform. Flinging on my leather jacket, I ventured out into the Sanctum.

The Tudor-style building was silent and layered with shadows, the various weapons displayed on the walls appeared menacing in the silver-tinted night. Halberds, arondight hilts, swords, spears, and shields made up the bulk of the medieval displays, but it was the eight-foot-tall marble statue of the Lady of the Lake that dominated the entire building.

I moved silently past her vacant eyes and climbed the stairs to the roof, though when I opened the door, I realised I wasn't alone.

Wilder sat on the edge of the building, his feet dangling over the lip of the gutter. I wasn't exactly annoyed he was up here, but I had hoped for a little alone time to deconstruct the new instalment in my dreamtime series.

"What are you doing up here?" I asked, sitting beside him.

He glanced up, but I knew he already sensed my

arrival before I'd even opened the door. After spending so much time together, he was able to tune into my channel with his ultra-Natural abilities.

"I should be asking the same thing," he said. "We've got training in a few hours."

"I couldn't sleep." I sighed and cast my gaze out over the city. "And this is as close to the outside world as I can get until my probation is lifted." I gave him some serious side-eye.

"Don't look at me like that."

"Greer said—"

"I know what Greer said," he interrupted. "You won't get any special treatment from me. You might've been touched by Arondight, but that doesn't make you all-powerful."

"Don't you wish it did, though?" I mused. "Wouldn't that be a trip?"

"I need to find a new spot," Wilder stated. "There's too much noise in this one."

"I'll be quiet," I promised a little too quickly.

"And here I was thinking you loathed my presence."

I snorted. Far from it, much to my annoyance.

"It's freezing out here," I said. There were some things that just needed to be left unsaid for the benefit of everyone.

"There'll be snow soon," he mused. "We haven't had any this year. It's strange."

"Wilder…" I let my words die in my throat, not sure how to tell him about my dream. It seemed important, and he was my mentor and trainer, but sometimes I didn't know how to talk to him. Especially in moments like these when he had his walls up.

"What is it, Purples? Spit it out." And there he went being all *sensitive*.

"I've got a bad feeling. Something…something's in my dreams."

He frowned, and I didn't like it. "Like what?"

"That night at *8-bit*…" I began to fiddle with the hem of my T-shirt. "The alley where we first met—"

"Don't remind me, Purples. You sucked a lot of Light out of me that night with your annoying immunity to alteration."

I snorted and punched him in the arm. "Jackson was there and a demon of some kind. A shadow that phased in and out."

Wilder scowled and shook his head. "It's just a dream."

"Was it? It felt important. He said the arondight blade wasn't fast enough. Whatever that means." My frown deepened. "What if he's in trouble?"

"Purples, you're just tired. People dream a lot when they're under stress. It happens."

"Are you sure?"

He grunted and turned back towards the city. London sparkled with orange and yellow artificial lights, and the Thames glittered as it flowed away from the sea, completely at the mercy of the tides.

"Wilder—"

"You better go back inside, Purples. There's only a few hours before the sun comes up."

His brush off wasn't unexpected, but it still hurt. Echoing his earlier grunt, I rose to my feet and walked away, too much on my mind to worry about Wilder's grumpy exterior.

He tended to be right about most things. It was another item on the list of his personality traits that annoyed me no end.

It was just a dream. Jackson was fine. He was a super-powered demon-hybrid on the side of the Light. He could protect himself.

*It was just a dream.*

## 3

As I expected, I was obliterated when I dragged myself out of bed the next morning.

I was drifting in and out of sleep, dangling dangerously over my bowl of bland muesli, when Romy sat down across from me. I jerked awake, flicking milk over the table.

"Careful, you don't want to drown in your cereal," she chirped, her eyes bright and alert.

"Don't sound so cheerful," I grumbled. "It's making my head ache."

She leaned forward and rested her chin on her hands. "What's up?"

"Wilder's on the grumpy warpath again," I said with a dramatic moan.

She shrugged. "That's Wilder."

My thoughts went back to last night and the way he brushed off my concerns about Jackson. "It wouldn't hurt him to be a little less dismissive, though."

"Yeah, but he's probably the best to learn from," Romy said. "Wilder's weird, doesn't like authority, and has an arrogant streak that makes him anti-social at best, but he was top of his class at the academy."

"Really?" I asked, suddenly interested. "He's never mentioned it."

The Natural shrugged. "His name was over everything. The honour roll, trophies, and medals, all that kind of stuff, but no one ever talked about him. Not really. It wasn't until I was assigned to the Sanctum that I understood why. I mean, people talked and passed around rumours about his funky eyes and stuff, but it never meant that much to me. Not until I saw him."

I snorted and resisted the urge to roll my eyes— eyes being the word of the day. "I wouldn't know the difference, really."

"Kids are cruel no matter what race they belong to," Romy said. "We're different, but when someone's different again… I guess we're also victims of fear, just like humans."

I couldn't even imagine what Wilder must've gone through at that school. His eyes had a silver sheen in certain light, much like a demon's did, and when you looked like the race of pure evil you were training to battle, that was an invitation for all kinds of awful stuff —bullies, hazing, ostracisation. He'd also confessed to me that his Natural abilities ran a little deeper than they were supposed to, which accounted for his obvious prodigy status at the academy. He must have been the height of popularity, *not*, but I could understand how it might've shaped his adult life. I could relate—I had my own quirks due to the same kind of experiences.

Chairs scraped back as we were joined by Martin, Alo, and Valeria, who all looked perfect in their own tough-as-nails Natural way. Alo grinned at me, and I couldn't help but smile back like a moron. His bulky muscles, long hair, and plaited beard gave him a mean metal-head look—sometimes it looked like he walked off the set of a movie about Vikings—but he was a big teddy bear underneath that aggressive demon hunter exterior.

"You look like shite," Martin declared. He was the high and mighty type, who was always quick to tell anyone how much he disliked Wilder. I wouldn't go as far to say he was a Natural purist, but his hatred for demons was on another level. It was clear something had happened in his past, though I wasn't asking any questions.

"Thanks," I shot back, digging my spoon into my muesli.

"Every time I see you in the gym, you're soaked with sweat," Valeria added. Sweet, ginger, Valeria with her freckles, willowy frame, and deadly twin arondight blades. I'd seen her train, too.

I shrugged. "I've got a lot of catching up to do."

Alo wrapped his hand around my bicep and squeezed. "You've got muscles, Scarlett. Actual muscles!"

"Smart-arse," I muttered, shaking him off as the others laughed.

"Just keep working at it," Romy said. "When you get used to it, stuff stops hurting."

"I hope so." I slumped over my breakfast. "Some days I can hardly sit down."

The Naturals were having a good laugh at my expense when Wilder appeared out of the ether and glowered down at us. He'd moved so silently that none of us had seen or heard him approach. *What a creeper.*

Martin scowled up at him, Alo gulped, Valeria openly stared, and Romy was indifferent to the intimidating glare of the six-foot-two demon hunter, but that was Romy. She was as easy-going as a warrior in an eternal fight between Light and Dark could get.

"Scarlett," Wilder said, ignoring the looks thrown his way. He said he was used to being ostracised by his own people, but I kind of felt enraged for him.

Uh oh, he was calling me by my name again, which meant I was either in trouble or something important was going down. I couldn't think of any rules I'd broken, so I hoped he was here because of the latter.

"See you guys later," I said, peeling myself away from the table.

We'd barely left the kitchen when I began to pepper him with questions.

"What's going on? Has something happened? Is it Jackson? Has someone found the Balan demon?"

I followed him through the halls and down a flight of stairs before he put me out of my misery and offered an explanation.

"We're going out into the city tonight," he said.

It was exactly what I wanted, but I found myself panicking over the thought of the battle being fought in the shadows. I'd faced demons before—lesser ones in the tube, Infernals in the street, and the Balan who'd infiltrated the Sanctum—so I shouldn't be afraid. Thinking about the demonology book Wilder had given me the other day, I shuddered. The difference from then to now was that I now understood what they were and all the ways they could eat my soul.

"But I haven't even started to use my Light yet," I whined. "What if—"

"You were the one who was complaining about not going after your boyfriend," Wilder stated. "Now that you've got the chance, you're afraid?"

"I'm not afraid and he's not my boyfriend."

"Oh, that's right. He was into monogamy and you were into playing both worlds."

I gasped. "You didn't just say that!"

He raised his eyebrows. "Come with me."

"Where are we going?"

"You'll see."

We were down in the basement, but not as far as the vaults. I wasn't keen on revisiting the cells below the Sanctum, so I was glad when we stopped outside a nondescript door.

Opening it, Wilder practically shoved me into the murky room beyond.

My eyes widened as I realised where we were. It was an entire room of arondight blades. They were all hilts of course, but I knew the power they concealed.

I walked around the room, my footsteps echoing back and forth against the flagstones. There were no two hilts alike. Some had heavy cross guards, others had forked counter weights, others were carved with elaborate designs, a few had jewelled pommels, and some were short while others were long. There were more modern designs that had cross guards that retracted down into the handgrips and were unadorned.

"There's so many," I said, my voice loud in the hushed armoury.

"There's eighty-two," Wilder stated. "London has the largest collection out of the other Sanctums."

"What about the ones on the walls?"

"Those are historical relics," he replied. "And some of them are blades of the fallen."

"Really? Why hasn't anyone told me?"

"You'd know if you read the nameplates." Wilder nodded towards the racks of arondight blades. "It's time to choose, Purples."

I swallowed hard and raked my gaze over the sword hilts. The role I'd fought so hard for was suddenly becoming real, and I wasn't prepared for the anxiety that rose in my gut. Once I chose a blade, that was it. I was not longer a Natural in probationary training…I was a *Natural*.

"Why now?" I asked, turning to face Wilder. "We've only been training for a month."

"Time isn't on our side, Purples." He didn't offer

any more explanation, and I curled my lip in annoyance.

I knew the stakes, but it was apparent something had changed. Recently, too.

"I'm getting my first arondight blade," I said to the empty room. "Somehow I feel like my parents should have been here."

"It isn't a ceremony," Wilder drawled. "There isn't cake after this. Just the fight against the Darkness."

"*Please*." I didn't need his smart-arse commentary, I needed my mentor. "What do I do?"

"Choose," he stated. "You'll know when you find the right one." He looked at his watch.

"Wilder, this is important. Can you quit the attitude for once in your life? I don't need the wounded guy with a chip on his shoulder, I need my mentor."

His jaw tightened. "Fine," he said, stepping into my personal space. Pressing his hands on my shoulders, he turned me around so my back was to him.

"Close your eyes," he murmured, his breath warm against the shell of my ear. "Listen."

I did as he said, the entire length of my body tingling from his closeness. It wasn't like all the times we tangled during training, it was something more intimate. This moment was more important than any other in my training, and Wilder's presence stirred something unknown inside me. I tensed, and his hands tightened on my shoulders.

"Close out everything else," he whispered. "Forget me. Forget why you're here. *Listen.*"

I lowered my head and breathed deeply, shutting out the physical distractions. We stood in the centre of the room for what felt like an age before I opened my eyes. Turning to the left, I shook off Wilder's touch and moved towards the rack of hilts.

*Which one are you?* I mused silently.

Reaching out, I picked up a simple unassuming hilt. The moment I held it firmly in my grasp, I knew it was mine. There was no fanfare, no zap of Light, no magical ta-da, there was just simple *knowledge*.

I held it out in front of me, marvelling at how light it was. The cross guard was small and curled in on itself, and the pommel was a twisted ball of metal that resembled a flickering flame caught by the wind. The grip was delicate but held enough roughness that my hands held firm.

It was nothing like the other arondight blades I'd used before. Those had been heavy and unwieldy, and even Wilder's was too bulky for me.

I turned to find Wilder smirking at me.

"I didn't hear anything," I said, wondering if I'd done it wrong. "I just knew."

His lips quirked. "That's how it's supposed to work, Purples." He took the hilt from my hands and turned it over, inspecting my choice. "Cool."

"Cool?"

"It's small, easily concealed, light, and good for your height and weight. The blade will be long and slim. It suits your style."

"It does?"

He pressed the hilt into my hands. "Give it a try."

The metal was cool in my palms, but my grip was steady, like it was made to be held by me and me alone.

Wilder gave me some space, and as I brought the blade to life, my Light tingled. Violet sparks erupted as the sword clicked into place—long and slim, just like Wilder said—and my eyes widened. This was my arondight blade. *Mine.*

"Congratulations," Wilder drawled. "You just passed your first test."

I hesitated. "Wait, that was a test?"

"Greer was worried you wouldn't be able to find one," he replied with a nonchalant shrug. "She thought you'd only be able to wield *the* Arondight."

I screwed up my nose. "That's silly. I've been able to use other blades just fine."

"You can use other blades, but they don't work as well as the one that chooses you." He gestured for me to sheath my sword.

"It chose me!" I grinned, realising what it meant. I was a true Natural despite my contact with Arondight and my tumultuous upbringing, including all those years of pills dampening my Light.

"Don't let it go to your head," Wilder said, rolling his eyes.

"What now?" I asked as I willed my blade to return to the hilt.

"Now we go find that weedy demon-hybrid and save him from himself."

After a whole day of stewing in my own juices, we'd left the Sanctum the moment night had fallen. The second Wilder and I had passed through the magical cloak over the building, I was disappointed to find my uneasiness didn't stay behind. I hadn't left London, but it felt like I was returning home after a long absence and someone had changed the carpet without me knowing.

The train carriage jolted, and I grasped the bright yellow pole, checking to make sure my arondight blade was still hidden inside my leather jacket. My nerves were getting the better of me and it had nothing to do with the possibility of running into a demon or two. When we found Jackson, what was I going to say to him?

'*Sup. We're here to take you back to the Sanctum where Ramona, the surly Natural doctor, wants to experiment on you to find out what makes you tick.*' Somehow, I was positive that wasn't the angle I should come at this from.

Wilder leaned against the pole in the middle of the carriage, his body swaying with the movement of the train as it zoomed through the underground. Commuters gave him a wide berth as they got on and off, unconsciously moving away from the sense of danger he exuded.

I studied everyone who passed, wondering if a demon was hitching a ride in any of their mortal shells. I couldn't tell, but maybe they were all clean.

"How do you know?" I asked, sidling up beside Wilder.

"Know what?" he drawled, looking bored.

"That something's in them," I replied. "The last time I was on the tube with you, you sensed one without even looking."

"When you're tuned to your Light, you'll be able to feel them."

I glowered, staring at our reflections in the windows as the tunnel flashed past. "That's why I was worried about coming out here without learning more about it."

"You're not alone anymore, Purples. You've got me."

I made a face. *Let's throw a party.* He grunted but didn't rise to my sarcastic baiting. "I don't even know what to tell Jackson." My frown deepened. "We've never fought like this."

"I'm fairly sure no one's had a falling out over being a demon-hybrid before."

"I don't care about that," I argued. "And that's not why we fell out."

"Pardon me," Wilder declared with a pout. "The poor guy was in unrequited love with the very person who'd just signed up to kill creatures like him."

"Sounds a lot like this silver-eyed arsehole I know."

"Low blow, Purples." He shifted his weight as the train began to slow for the next station. "If he's as important to you as you say he is, then you already know what to tell him."

The doors swished open and the speakers blared, *'This station is Camden Town, Edgware branch. Change here for all stations to High Barnet and Mill Hill East from platform three. This train terminates at Edgware.'*

Wilder strode off the train and onto the platform with me on his heels. We worked our way through the narrow tunnels and rode the escalator to the surface.

I noticed we weren't jostled once, even though there was a thick crowd heading out for the night. Camden was always pumping, especially once everyone knocked off work for the day. There were tons of pubs, clubs, restaurants, and live music venues drawing people who were looking for a bit of fun from all over the city.

When we walked out of the station, I was surprised when we turned up the High Street and not towards Kentish Town Road, where Jackson's flat was located.

"Where are we going?" I asked, jogging to catch up to Wilder.

"The child care centre you call a pub," he replied, weaving past a group of rowdy punks.

"*8-bit?*" I choked a little on my spit. I hadn't even given notice that I was quitting, I just never showed up for work like the irresponsible delinquent I'd been as a teenager, and now Wilder wanted me to go back there? I already felt the flames of embarrassment creeping onto my cheeks.

"Suck it up, Purples, they don't remember you."

"They what?" I tugged at his sleeve. "You did a

mass alteration mind-wipe thing on the entire staff, didn't you?"

"Not me," he replied, "but yes."

"Why?" I cried. "You just erased me out of their lives!"

"It's safer for them this way," Wilder shot back, his brow creased with annoyance. "The less they know about you, the better."

"Do you understand how invasive that is? You can't just take away someone's memories without their permission!"

Wilder snarled and turned on his heel. I almost smacked into him, but his hand shot out and grasped my shoulder. "Listen up, Purples. You're the only person alive who's come into contact with Arondight in a thousand years—the one thing that could wipe out an entire race and end the war—and you think those humans would be safe to go about their lives unbothered by demons? How long do you think they'd last before they were possessed and tortured?"

"I-I…" I stammered, hardly aware of the people moving around us.

"We're not here to lord it over humanity," he added. "We're here to save them, Purples."

"I'm sorry, I didn't—"

"I would have liked to keep you in training for another six months at least, but here we are. I'd prefer it if you didn't get all up in my face about Natural business on a public street."

My mouth dropped open. "Six months?"

"That's the fast track, Purples."

"And what's this we're doing then?"

"*Desperation.*" He stalked off, leaving me to run to catch up yet again.

"My dream wasn't just a dream, was it?" I asked, falling into stride beside him.

"We think the demons are going to make a move on him," Wilder confirmed. "We're not the only ones who've been watching."

And I was the only one who had a chance to convince him to come without a fight. I understood that it was more to do with Jackson's unpredictable hybrid status than our past relationship. Sure, it didn't hurt that he was the closest thing to a family I'd had in recent years, but no one had been mutated by an Infernal before.

*8-bit* was pumping when we walked in the front door. The arcades were full, people were lounging on the couches with pints in their hands, cosplayers were taking selfies, the bar was packed, and music was blaring. It was a typical Saturday dance party in this place.

I craned my neck, searching for Jackson.

"Are you sure he's here?" I shouted at Wilder.

When he began to laugh at something across the pub, I scowled and followed his gaze. I froze when I caught sight of a familiar head of curly hair.

Jackson was leaning against the bar, a woman dressed in a revealing video game character costume draped over his startlingly muscular body. She pressed her lips against his and they began to suck some serious face. When his hands went for her arse, I turned away.

Wilder snorted, not doing the best job of hiding his amusement. "Yeah, looks like he's pining over you big time, Purples."

**4**

———

"You might want to go pry them apart with a crowbar," Wilder said, gesturing across the pub to where Jackson was enthusiastically kissing some random cosplayer. "They look like they'll be at it for a while."

I couldn't look at them.

"What happened to him?" I asked, shaking my head. "He's different."

"I'd say it's his mutation," Wilder replied. "It fixed his eyesight, so it'd stand to reason it'd give him other advantages, too. Demons can be excessively fast, strong, and their reflexes are sharp."

I thought back to the e-sports tournament Jackson had won and nodded. He'd been able to anticipate his opponent's moves and react within hundredths of a second. His mutation still seemed to be manifesting, even though Ramona had assured us she'd halted the process.

His smirk widened as Jackson went in for a grope. "We haven't got all night, Purples."

Sucking up my embarrassment, I stalked through *8-bit*, dodging drunken cosplayers. I still didn't know what to say and interrupting his sloppy make-out session was not how I envisioned our first encounter after *that* argument played out.

I stood next to them and scowled when they didn't even surface. I stared, silently willing for someone to notice me before I imploded. It was really starting to get uncomfortable with all the tongue and kissy sounds.

Knowing Wilder was watching, I glowered and tapped Jackson on the shoulder. He didn't seem to notice, so I shoved him as hard as I could.

They broke apart and the woman glared at me while Jackson began to pale.

"Hey!" she exclaimed, her cleavage spilling out of an extremely low-cut top. "What's your problem?"

Jackson looked startled for a moment, then said, "Go away, Scarlett."

"Is that all you've got to say to me?" I demanded.

"And who the hell are you?" the woman asked, getting all hoity-toity.

I ignored her, which only seemed to make her angrier. "I need to talk to you," I said to Jackson, "it's important."

"We're busy, if you can't tell," the woman said, rubbing her palms over his chest.

*Puke.* "Take a hike," I snarled at her.

Something dangerous must've flashed in my eyes because she balked and backed away.

"Nice going, Scarlett," Jackson drawled, picking up the pint that was behind him on the bar.

"I need to talk to you."

"You're only here because you want something."

"That's not true!"

He rolled his eyes and downed the last of his beer. "Save it for someone who cares, Scarlett."

"Jackson, there's something out there trying to turn innocent humans into demons. You could help stop that from happening." I grabbed the front of his shirt and shoved him down into a free chair behind him. "We're *asking* for your help."

His eyes widened at my aggressive shove and I sat across from him, hyperaware that Wilder was sniggering behind me.

"All this time, you've been out here sleeping around and flaunting your new abilities?" I demanded. "That's not you, Jackson."

"How would you know?" he asked, narrowing his eyes. "You're the one who dumped me."

"You told me not to come after you!" I exclaimed.

"Everyone knows you're supposed to ignore it when people say that," he said sullenly.

"And you know how socially awkward I can get with these things," I fired back. "It's not like we're in an everyday scenario here."

He glared over my shoulder at Wilder, clearly not impressed by my company.

"After you left, I went after the Infernal who

possessed you," I blurted. "But I screwed up, Jackson. I almost got myself killed, and I pulled Romy and Martin into an unnecessary fight. I got into serious trouble. If I wanted to continue training, I couldn't leave. Then the Sanctum was attacked and—"

"The Sanctum was attacked?" he asked, looking troubled. "When?"

"About a month ago."

"And you didn't tell me?"

"I just said I couldn't leave, and I don't have a phone anymore. I'm just a trainee, it's not like I'm told everything that's going on."

"And you want me to go with you? You're just a disposable solider in their war, Scarlett. What do you think they're going to do to me if I go back? Are they really just going to take a few blood samples and do a few tests? Or are they going to crack open my chest and do a live autopsy against my will?"

"I trust Greer," I replied firmly. "I didn't before, but now I know she wants to set things right with what happened to you. If there's something they can learn about your DNA—"

"Time's up," Wilder said grabbing Jackson's arm. "There's no more time for arguing the finer points of supernatural politics. We've got to get out of here."

"Let me go," Jackson snarled, wrenching his arm away from the Natural.

"Get it through your head, nerdelinger. They're watching you. Once they know we're here, they'll make their play and it won't be pretty. Either you come with us, or you go with them."

"What's a nerdelinger?" I asked.

"The ultimate nerd," Wilder replied, glaring at Jackson. "What's it going to be? Light or Dark?"

"Wilder!" I exclaimed.

"We're out of time," he snarled. "We need to go. *Now*."

"They're here?" Jackson swallowed hard.

"They want their science project back," the Natural stated. "It was only a matter of time."

"We're trying to help you," I said, starting to become jittery. "I want to stop my best friend from being captured by demons and save innocent people. Will you come with us?"

"Me?" He snorted. "I'm not important. I—"

"*Jackson*." I didn't know what else to say, so I pleaded with my eyes.

A tense moment of silence that stretched between us. The music was blaring, people were dancing amongst the flashing lights, and we sat amidst it, talking about demons and mutations like they were everyday occurrences.

"All right," Jackson said after a moment, "I'll come back with you. If I'm the only one who can help stop people from turning into demons, then I suppose I couldn't live with myself if I did nothing."

"Good." Wilder shoved him out of his chair and jostled him through the crowd.

I chased after the two men with an annoyed scowl. It wouldn't hurt Wilder to be a little nicer about things—it'd go a long way in helping people actually like him more. The door swung closed in my face and I cursed under my breath. Like I was saying…

Pushing out on to the street, I froze as I stared right into the face of a demon. The man, who was possessed up the wazoo, flashed me a toothy grin. His eyes flashed silver and instead of grabbing him, I hesitated.

"*Arondight*," it said. "*Surprise!*"

Its body coiled, gathering its strength to lunge at me, but Wilder was there, shoving it against the wall.

"Scarlett!" Jackson cried, reaching for me.

The demon's head turned with unnatural speed, looking between the three of us, then it broke free from Wilder's grasp and bolted down the street.

"Why is it running?" I asked.

"It knows its outmatched," Wilder replied with a snarl.

He threw up his arm and I felt his Light envelop all three of us, then he sprinted after the creature, weaving through the mass of people walking up and down the footpath. No one paid him any attention, which explained a lot. I'd never known this world existed until the night I'd seen through Wilder's cloaking, and for good reason. If the public knew about demons and the Naturals, there'd be mass hysteria.

Cursing, I grabbed Jackson's hand and took off after Wilder and the demon.

"Scarlett!" Jackson called. "What are you doing?"

"*My job.*"

The markets were open late tonight for a

Christmas-themed event, and there were tourists and locals swarming the shops and stalls browsing. The hustle and bustle gave the demon all the advantage as it twisted and turned in an attempt to shake us off its tail.

Wilder pushed a random stranger out of the way, and Jackson and I were left to weave around their angry ranting at an innocent passer-by. We crossed the street, dodging traffic, then weaving all over the footpath and the road.

As my boots thudded on the flagstones, I wondered if this was how Wilder usually conducted his demon hunts. It didn't seem the preferable option, given the overpopulation of this part of the city.

Ahead, the demon grabbed at a stand of bootleg T-shirts and pulled it down across the footpath, sending cheap material and plastic-coated racks in all directions. People cried out and scattered as the heavy racks clattered across the ground. Wilder skidded and bashed into a man before dodging the rest of the chaos and following the demon into the tight warren of clothing stalls near the tube station.

Jackson and I passed the startled man a second later. He stumbled and looked left and right, but couldn't see the purple-haired demon hunter and her hybrid friend sprint past.

I turned into the tight walkway, jostling past shoppers in my desperation to find Wilder and the demon, but we'd lost them amongst the tight maze of clothes and jewellery. We turned another corner, only to find the same scene of polyester and more polyester before us.

"*Shit*," I cursed.

"Where did they go?" Jackson asked, swatting away an ugly skirt that was flapping in his face.

I stepped aside as a group of tourists came towards us. As they passed, they seemed to stare straight through us, which meant Wilder's Light was still cloaking us. They were close.

"They're around here somewhere," I murmured, reaching for my cold iron dagger that was concealed in a sheath inside my boot.

"What the hell is that?" Jackson asked, eyeing the gunmetal-coloured blade.

"*Shh.*" I pressed my finger to my lips. "Stay close."

I called on the things I'd learned in training as I scanned the area directly around us. Wilder shouldn't have left me, but I hadn't been quick enough to keep up, and now we were separated in a confusing maze of cheaply made alternative clothing and cut-price silicone body jewellery—and I had no idea how to use my Light without risking soul sickness.

There was no use agonising over it now.

I edged forwards with Jackson bridging up the rear. Everywhere I looked were smiling faces and I expected their eyes to shine silver in the muted lighting, but they were all human. Innocents that were about to be caught up in an epic game of cat and mouse. If the demon decided to jump bodies, we were screwed.

We turned down another row of stalls, and

somewhere I sensed Wilder doing the same. If I could sense him with my untrained abilities, maybe he could do the same. It meant he hadn't run off on us after all, thought I wasn't feeling reassured about it right at this very moment.

I detected a sharp movement to my right just as a rack of clothing exploded. The demon erupted out of the mass of polyester and lycra and lunged at us with terrifying speed. It let out a shriek that seemed to tear its throat apart as the oblivious stall holder cried out in surprise.

I reacted instantly, relying on the training Wilder had been beating into my skull over the past month, and pushed towards the wall of flesh. I thrust the dagger upwards, hardly aware of Jackson's startled shouts behind me. The demon rolled to the side, glancing off my shoulder, and I was jerked off balance. Falling back on my heel, the creature's unnatural strength forced me to my knees.

Behind me, Jackson collided with the demon and shoved it back the way it'd came. His expression morphed into shock as he began to realise the true strength his mutation had granted him. It was just like Romona and everyone else had suspected.

Unfortunately, I didn't have time to dwell on the particulars as the man hurtled straight at me. Pushing off the ground, I drove the dagger towards the demon. The blade imbedded into its chest with a thud, only stopping when the cross guard collided with flesh.

The man wailed and collapsed, pulling me down on top of his thrashing body.

It happened so fast, I didn't see Wilder barrel through the stalls. He skidded to his knees beside me and held down the demon's arms as I straddled it, twisting the cold iron dagger in an attempt to pry out the parasite. Jackson followed his lead and grabbed its feet, steadying the writhing mass of flesh.

"It's not leaving," I cried. "*It's still in there.*"

Wilder grasped the demon's face and checked its eyes. "What do you want with the hybrid?" he demanded. "Tell us and we'll go easy on you."

"He's ours," the demon rasped, its eyes flashing silver. "*Ours.*"

"I'm not anyone's!" Jackson exclaimed.

"You're a demon," the creature cried. "Darkness flows in your veins. Back blood. Black blood. *Black blood!*"

"Black blood?"

"Don't listen to it," I said. "It's trying to screw with you."

"Screw, screw, screw!" the demon shouted, then began to laugh hysterically. It shook its head back and forth, letting out an unearthly howl.

"It's not going to tell us shit," Wilder said. "We have to excise and kill it before it does more harm."

"But I've never done an exorcism before," I cried.

"Consider this a crash course." He wrenched the cold iron dagger out of the man's chest, causing the demon to shriek.

It shook its hosts head back and forth, sending spit

flying. "I've eaten his soul," it chortled, smacking its lips together. "*Mmmmm! Tasty!* I can't wait to eat yours, Natural."

"*Gross*," I hissed, trying not to puke as Jackson and Wilder held it down.

Wilder grabbed my hand and pressed it against the demon's chest, then flattened his palm over mine.

"Follow my lead and you'll do fine," Wilder said.

"But my Light—"

"*Prize et mortale, hoc a te carnem*," he chanted, his gaze fixed on mine. "Scarlett! Say the words!"

"*Prize et mortale, hoc a te carnem*," I echoed, my entire body shaking.

"*Habes imperium terrae*," he went on, and I followed his lead, my tongue thick with the unfamiliar words. "*Hanc lucem mortales proficeret.*" I felt my power flare and the demon began to wail, the sound inhuman to my ears. "*Lucius Annaeus Seneca. Lucius Annaeus Seneca. Lucius Annaeus Seneca.*"

The man's mouth gaped and inky black smoke poured out of him and into the air. Wilder let my hand go, and in one swift movement, he flipped his arondight blade into his palm and it erupted in a shower of sparks as it tore through the excised demon.

The resulting explosion was a dull affair. It went *poof* like two chalkboard dusters being slapped together and sent out a shockwave that rattled the surrounding stalls.

Human heads turned towards the commotion, but the scene was met with confused stares. We'd just fought a demon and performed an exorcism in the middle of Camden Market while invisible. Clearly, it was going to take some time to get used to the whole cloaked thing.

"There was no way they didn't hear that thing screaming," Jackson stated.

"Don't patronise me," Wilder drawled, sheathing his arondight blade.

"How didn't you set anything on fire with that thing?" my best friend went on, his mouth running off as I climbed to my feet. "And you stabbed him in the chest!"

"If you took the time to notice rather than piss your pants, you would've seen that there was no blood." Wilder rolled his eyes and pulled an auto syringe from his inside jacket pocket. He pulled down the front of the man's T-shirt and stabbed the needle into his chest.

"And now you're drugging him!" Jackson exclaimed. "Scarlett, you can't be serious!"

"He knows what he's doing," I said, placing my hand on his shoulder.

"It ate part of his soul," Wilder said. "Show a little sympathy for your fellow possessed."

"It ate his soul? But——"

"He'll be fine." Wilder glared at him. "He'll wander out of here and reappear farther down the street, none the wiser about where he's been, with his soul fully intact."

"What if it was one of the DNA-altering kind?"

"You were different." Wilder stood and hauled the man up and dusted him off. The human teetered on his feet like he was drunk and blinked a few times.

"Where am I?" he asked with a groan.

"I think you've had a bit too much to drink," the Natural said. "You passed out, you poor sod. You better head home and sleep it off."

I could feel the tinge of Light weaving around the mortal's head and I glanced at Wilder. He was planting a suggestion into the guy's mind to get him home safe. Wilder could be grumpy and the biggest arsehole out there, but at least he cared about his duties as a Natural.

The man rubbed his eyes, then blinked. Turning around, he looked confused for a moment, then wandered off past the stands of clothing, became tangled in a maxi dress, then disappeared into the crowd.

Wilder handed me back my cold iron dagger and gestured for us to follow him. "We better get back to the Sanctum before his mates come looking for him."

"It's going to be an extended stay, isn't it?" Jackson asked, raking his hand through his curly mop of hair.

"Let's face it, there isn't any room service, but at least you aren't going to be charged a premium rate per night." The demon hunter stalked off, leaving us to jog to catch up with his long stride.

"You can learn more about your abilities and how to spot demons," I said as we melted through the city towards the tube station. "At least there's that."

"And how to fight them." Jackson gestured back to the market. "I was useless back there."

"It'd be good to have some company training. Maybe—"

"*No*," Wilder snarled, glaring at us.

"That guy's got issues," Jackson whispered into my ear. I knew Wilder heard him when I saw his shoulders tense.

We rode the tube back to Vauxhall in silence.

I didn't know what to focus on at first—my first exorcism, my best friend's transformation, or all the things that went wrong with our mission. It wasn't exactly smooth sailing. No doubt I'd get a thorough debriefing when we got back to the Sanctum.

It was almost midnight by the time we resurfaced on the south side of the Thames.

As we walked down the darkened street, Jackson glanced nervously between me and Wilder's hulking back in front of us. He was clearly at a loss for what to say to me, which broke my heart.

As we approached the Sanctum, I began to stew over all the regrets I'd amassed since finding my true heritage. It would've been easier on all of us if I'd felt the same way about Jackson as he had me, but I couldn't choose who I loved. I was pretty sure it didn't work that way.

Now things would never be the same between us and I longed for the easy friendship we'd had. I could tell Jackson anything, but it wasn't only that—he was the first person to actually listen to me…and stick around afterwards. He was my only family.

I tugged on my best friend's sleeve. "I'm sorry, Jackson."

He turned. "For?"

I shrugged, my cheeks heating. "For not returning your feelings."

Wilder glanced over his shoulder and narrowed his eyes. Then he moved farther down the street, giving us some space to talk. I stared at his broad shoulders and sighed as he melted into the shadows.

"He kiss you again?" Jackson asked, following my gaze.

"No." My thoughts went back to that night outside my room and the brief, yet shattering kiss Wilder and I had shared. "Honestly, I don't even know what happened for it to be a thing the first time."

"So you're not—"

"He's got a thing for Greer," I said, scraping my hair behind my ear, "besides, he's my mentor."

"Wow, lucky you. How did you get lumped with that?"

"It's a mystery for the ages," I replied with a roll of my eyes. "I think it has something to do with his surly rigidness dampening my reckless need to rush into danger and cut down demons with my sharp wit."

"It looks like a lot of things have happened," he said awkwardly. "You look…stronger."

"So do you," I replied. "You've got game."

His lips quirked, and the air began to warm a little between us.

"Jackson—"

"I know what you're going to say," he said before I

could formulate my chaotic thoughts. "You can't choose these things, and you can't control what comes back."

I nodded. "I wish…"

"So do I," he murmured. "So do I."

5

---

J ackson's arrival at the Sanctum this time was more welcoming than the last. Though he set off the alarms again, our arrival was expected, and Romy was there to throw the switch when we crossed the threshold.

"Oh, you've changed," she'd declared as she laid eyes on my best friend.

"Thanks for noticing," he'd replied with a wink.

Greer had assigned Jackson his own room, so I went to find him the next morning, but found it empty.

Swinging by the kitchen, he wasn't there either. When I got to the infirmary, I saw him inside, a team of Naturals flocking around him like hungry seagulls fighting over a hot chip.

I caught his gaze and lifted my hand in a wave. He grimaced, drawing the ire of Ramona, who shooed me away.

Wilder was waiting for me when I got to the gym.

I wondered if Jackson was okay, and what tests Ramona was going to do. At least he had his own room this time and wasn't locked up in the vaults like a prisoner. Though even I wasn't naïve enough to believe he wasn't being watched at all times.

"You're doing that overthinking thing again," Wilder stated while he kicked off his boots.

"I'm worried." I followed suit, taking off my boots and stuffing my socks inside. "I know I'm just a soldier and I'm not supposed to ask questions, but why now?"

"Why go pick up your man-friend?"

"Yeah."

Choosing his words carefully, Wilder replied, "Demon activity has been increasing."

I lowered my gaze and nodded. "Because of me?"

"You're the only thing that's changed."

After a lifetime of being unimportant, I wasn't really comfortable being the centre of attention. Though, being in the spotlight with the Naturals meant they gave me side-eye while plotting secret meetings I wasn't invited to.

"If I'm so important then why can't I know what's going on?"

"There's a hierarchy, Purples. I'm not immune to it, and neither are you."

I stared at my toes and scowled. "I don't like it."

"Neither do I, but you already know about my dislike for authority."

I looked up. "What's that supposed to mean?"

"Exactly what you think it means," he replied with a shrug.

I was getting the feeling he wanted me to bypass the chain of command and do things Wilder-style, but I wasn't about to do anything to screw up my chances of getting my probation lifted. Maybe in time, when I knew how far I could stretch the limits of the higher up's orders, I would tap into my inner-Wilder.

"If I'm cleared for duty, then we can do our own digging." I sat on the mat and began to stretch and loosen my muscles.

"It's likely Brax will ask me to keep an eye on you," Wilder said, joining me.

I snorted, not bothering to cover up my dislike for the only other man in the entire Sanctum who was more abrasive than Wilder. Unfortunately, he was in a power position as one of the three heads of the whole operation in London, so at some point, I had to answer to him.

"So, if I go out on patrol, I'll be doing that whole bait thing again?"

"Not necessarily, but they have to lure out that Balan demon somehow." *The demon who killed my parents…*

"There are still no leads?"

"Everyone's on the lookout, but there's not enough of us," Wilder said. "We're spread far too thin to be able to cover all that ground. Even if there wasn't an increased threat level, we still can't protect the entirety of London."

It seemed to frustrate him, and I offered him a weak smile.

"We do what we can." Gesturing to myself, I added, "Then there's lavender bait."

He grunted and pressed his bare feet against mine. Reaching out, he grasped my wrists, and I wrapped my fingers around his, and he helped me stretch.

"You did good last night, Purples," he said, pulling back.

"Is that a compliment I hear?" I declared with a smirk.

His lips quirked. "Don't get used to it."

I wanted to ask him if he'd heard anything about Jackson, but now didn't seem like the right time. Not while Wilder had a direct view down my cleavage.

"That exorcism…" I began, following another train of thought, "that was Latin, wasn't it?"

He nodded.

"What does it mean in English?"

I pulled back against his grasp as he translated, "I prise you from this mortal flesh, you have no dominion on Ear, let Light prevail over this mortal soul. Begone, begone, begone." He grunted. "It's sounds a bit too much like religious dogma, but it works."

"I felt my Light stir."

"It's not so much the words as the Light," he confirmed.

"Then why say them at all?"

"It pisses off the demons."

I frowned. "Really?"

"Latin seems to be something close to their native

language," he explained. "That's what people think anyway. The words are a conduit for our Light to travel and do what it's told."

"Like a lightning rod?"

"Words have their own kind of power," he replied mysteriously.

"I'm so far behind," I said with a moan. I'd missed out on so many things, and I wondered if I would always be playing catch up.

"You're doing okay, Purples. You pick up things quickly."

"Really?"

"You made it quite clear last night." He gave me a pointed look before he said, "You didn't hesitate."

"I did when it came time for the exorcism."

"No, I mean with the dagger. You were right to hold back during the exorcism. You don't have the training to use your Light on your own yet."

Whenever that was. Light was a huge part of who I was, and not knowing how to draw on it frustrated me more than I cared to admit. I bet Wilder didn't have this problem. He grew up knowing what he was —to a certain degree—and had all the associated training and experience. Suddenly, I felt envious.

"You've got that look again," Wilder drawled.

"What was it like…you know, growing up a Natural?" I asked, carefully gauging his reaction. I knew he didn't like to talk about himself, but he knew pretty much everything about me. Well, all the important bits anyway.

He shrugged and let me go. Drawing his knees back, he sat cross-legged and scowled.

"That good, huh?"

"I don't like talking about it."

"I know. I can tell you an embarrassing story about my past, if it makes you feel more comfortable."

"Knowing you, I think I'll pass."

"*Pfft.*" I rolled my eyes but was kind of glad he didn't follow up on it. Otherwise, he'd have fodder to tease me with later. "What about your family? Do you keep in touch?"

"I don't have any family."

I hesitated. "What? None at all?"

He shook his head, a haunted look passed across his features.

"What about your parents?" I prodded.

"I never had any."

It was in that moment that I realised I knew exactly zero about the man who was my mentor, trainer, and most trusted confidant inside the strange world of the Naturals. There'd always be this wall between us—the wall that kept any romance from blooming—but he was the guy who was shaping me into the warrior I was destined to be. It felt important to return the favour.

Shocked by his admission, I whispered, "Never?"

"For as long as I remember, I was the kid who grew up at the academy," he said, his eyes flashing silver. "I don't know where I came from. I had nobody to go home to on holidays, so when the academy emptied out, I trained."

"I'm so sorry—"

"It's not important. I can't miss what I never had." Clearly, it was, but I knew better than to push, especially when he was the boss and I was the trainee.

"I was always bouncing around foster homes," I said. "Some were better than others, but better wasn't necessarily a cakewalk, either."

"How did you not realise your Light was manifesting?"

"How was I supposed to know?" I asked. "I didn't even know what it felt like. I was angry a lot, got into fights… I was put on medication for my 'illness' in my early teens, and I struggled with pretty much everything. I ran away from a family or two, and I got arrested once. That scared me enough to straighten out."

"You were a real troublemaker, Purples," Wilder said. "That explains a lot."

"I always thought I was acting out because of my parents. There were times I hated them for leaving me, but mostly, I hated myself for being so screwed up. I just couldn't get it together."

Wilder eyed me. "So what changed?"

"I don't know." I shrugged. "I grew up, I suppose. I met Jackson and he gave a shit. Even when I fought with him, he stuck around. No one had ever done that for me, you know? He helped me get a job at *8-bit*, let me rent a room at his place… After a few years, things shifted." I laughed and shook my head. "Then I met you."

Wilder was silent a long time and I wondered if I should stay still in case I spooked him. This was another facet of him I'd never seen, and I found myself wanting to dig deeper.

"Come here." He gestured for me to sit directly in front of him and I hesitated. "I'm not going to bite, Purples. Though I can call down to Ramona and see if your hybrid man-friend is free."

It didn't take long for the surly Wilder to come back and I screwed up my face. The moment had passed and who knew when or if another would roll around.

I slid my arse across the floor and sat in front of him, but apparently, I wasn't close enough. He edged forward until our knees touched, then he held out his hands.

"What are you doing?" I asked, my voice breaking slightly.

He turned his hands so his palms were facing up. "Showing you the right way to reach for your Light."

*Oh…* I slid my hands into his, the gesture feeling a little too close for comfort. We kept having these moments and after everything that'd happened between us, I was entirely sure they were one-sided.

"Are you sure we aren't moving too fast?" I whispered.

He leaned closer and I sucked in a sharp breath.

"Why are you whispering?" He smirked, and I jerked my hands away and slapped him on the arm.

"*Wilder.*"

"It's like I said, Purples, we're out of time. The demons won't wait, and neither will we. You need to be ready to fight."

I slumped my shoulders. "Way to pile on the pressure."

Wilder grabbed my hands and pulled my focus back to him. "You're doing fine. Believe it, Purples. You've been fighting all your life, so this comes natural to you. Now," his grip tightened, "focus and listen."

I did as he said, but all I could hear was the sounds of the other Naturals training in the gym outside our private room. The whirr of machines, the clash of arondight blades, the cries of fighters colliding. I shook my head, trying to clear the distractions.

"Close your eyes," Wilder murmured.

Light played through my eyelids and I searched for the spark of power inside me. I'd used it before, but those times had been instinctual—and I'd been in life or death situations. Now I was attempting to call on it in a controlled environment, and it didn't want to stir.

"This is impossible." I let out a frustrated cry and Wilder tightened his hold on me.

"It's in you, Purples. The way isn't always easy, but there is always a way."

Closing my eyes again, I evened out my breathing and focused on shutting out the surrounding sounds. Then my thoughts began to kick into overdrive, but I shut them out, too. After a while, my head began to loll.

"Don't fall asleep," Wilder said with a chuckle. "You're not meditating, you're searching for something. Got it?" *When he said it like that...* "Let me guide you, Purples. I'll show you the first step."

He flexed his fingers, flattening his palms against mine. Then, in the darkness, I caught a glimpse of a silver spark as it sputtered into life.

"Is that you?" I asked.

"*Shh...*"

It was when I realised I was looking at him, not me, that things began to happen.

Warmth bloomed inside me, melting a strange pattern through my body. It was nowhere and everywhere all at the same time, ebbing and flowing with each pump of my heart. Indigo Light reached out towards Wilder's silver, flowing through our joined hands, flaring as his spark replied. It was exactly like the night we'd kissed and—

A surge of power zapped through me and I tore my hands from his. My eyes flew open and I stared into Wilder's startled gaze. Something told me that wasn't normal.

"Is that supposed to happen?" I whispered. "Our Light—"

The door opened, and I jerked backwards as Romy walked into the room. She glanced between Wilder and me, her eyebrows rising as she studied our closeness.

"Ramona would like to see you both in the

infirmary," she said before she flashed me a knowing look.

"What?" I demanded with a scowl.

"The infirmary," she repeated, her lips curving in amusement. "It's to do with Jackson."

"We'll be right there," Wilder said, not taking his eyes off me.

Romy chuckled to herself and left, closing the door behind her.

"Wilder—"

"You'll have to be careful with your Light," he interrupted, climbing to his feet. Sitting on the bench, he retrieved his socks and stuffed his feet into them. "I suspected it might be the case, so we're going to have to be more careful."

"Do you think I could hurt you?"

"Maybe... I don't really know."

I sighed and crawled across the mats to where I'd left my boots.

"It's not a bad thing, Purples. We're just in uncharted territory, is all."

"Sure." I pulled on my socks and shoved my feet into my boots. "How did that work out for you?"

I was beginning to get a deeper understanding of why Greer, Aldrich, and Brax assigned Wilder as my mentor—a lot of what he was, was unknown, too. We were the same, although we were on opposite sides of the same coin.

He snorted. "People assume I have demon heritage, while you were blessed by our most sacred relic."

"Okay." I held up my hands, feeling bad. "I retract my last smart-arse statement."

"Let's go find Ramona," Wilder said with a scowl. "We can try your Light again later."

As he stalked from the room, I scratched my head sheepishly. Why was I always sticking my foot in it?

## 6

Ramona was running tests in a laboratory that sat alongside the infirmary. When we entered, I was surprised to find all kinds of high-tech equipment scattered around the room. I had no idea what any of it did, but it looked fancy...and expensive.

Jackson was sitting on a chair with electrodes stuck to his bare chest and temples. Wires ran from each little circle into a machine that Ramona was studying intently.

"Hey!" he said when he saw us.

I looked him over, the weedy gamer guy I'd always known nowhere in sight. "Jackson... *You've got abs.*"

Wilder snorted behind me.

"I know, right?" Jackson grinned and slapped his stomach. "There's a first for everything."

"There you are," Ramona said, lifting her head. "We've barely gotten started, but there's already so much interesting data." She picked up a tablet and began to tap on the screen. "There's a great deal we don't know about the genetic and biological makeup of demons, but this is helping a great deal."

"You've captured them before, right?" I asked. "Haven't you been able to find anything out then?"

"It's difficult as most demons we're able to contain are made up of a dark, vaporous essence. They're not exactly easy to study."

"And others burst into flame when we kill them," Wilder said.

"Even their hierarchy and social structure is a mystery," Ramona added. "We used to believe they were simple-minded creatures with a fixed purpose. Now, we know they're so much more complex than we gave them credit for."

I glanced at Jackson. "So you're playing an epic game of catch up?"

She smiled. "Exactly."

I'd always known Ramona to be surly and ultra-focused on her work, but she seemed to be more comfortable, even excitable, in her natural habitat. It was wondrous to see a smile on her face for a change.

"What have you found out?" Wilder asked. "It must be important if you're interrupting our training."

Her trademark scowl quickly returned. "Watch your tone with me. Or the next time you're cut open by a demon, I won't be as careful with my stitching."

He raised an eyebrow.

Ignoring him, Ramona flipped over her tablet so we could see some test results. It was a full body scan, showing bones and internal organs, but there was a little extra thanks to the mutation. Black splotches scattered in various parts of his extremities with one red growth blooming in the centre of Jackson's chest.

"Here," she said, pointing to the crimson mass. "When I stopped the mutation, it hadn't completely settled into the host."

"She calls me 'the host'," Jackson said to me with a sigh. "I gotta tell ya, it's a real confidence booster."

"Those parts have remained active, which is why he's continued to change," she went on. "See how it pulsates?" She tapped on the screen and the scan began to move, the red splotch beating as if it were a second heart. "It's acting like an engine for his abilities. When we last saw him, his physique was leaner and his senses weren't as sharp. We've conducted hearing tests that indicate he can decipher sound in a range outside of the normal human spectrum."

He snorted. "That's a polite way of saying I can hear high-pitched sounds like a dog."

I smiled and patted him on the shoulder.

"These are all physical attributes," Wilder said, his eyes narrowing slightly. "What about his mind?"

"The mutation was designed to take over his entire body," Ramona replied. "Left untreated, this red mass would have grown until it changed his DNA entirely. It appears it never reached as far as the brainstem, but I am dealing with more unknowns than knowns at the moment. This Human Convergence Project seems to be highly experimental.

When I first encountered the altered cells, it was unlike anything I'd ever seen—crude, hasty, and a little desperate."

"The demons would only launch an unfinished weapon if they felt threatened," Wilder mused, looking over Ramona's research. "It's not like they didn't have time to perfect it. Not until—" He looked at me.

"Arondight." Ramona finished his thought.

*And it always comes back to me.* I sighed and offered Jackson a reassuring smile.

"It's not so bad," I said. "It's not like you're an actual demon or anything."

"Thank God my brainstem is still human," Jackson drawled. "Some of me still is a little demonic though. I keep setting off the alarms."

"Have you done any direct tests on the mass?" Wilder asked. "Nerve simulation? Light manifestations?"

"Not yet, though we've only been at this for a morning. I hope to compile an accurate map of where this mass has extended, then conduct some simulations for retraction."

"Retraction?" Jackson squeaked. "You're not going to try to cut me open, are you?"

"Of course not," Ramona replied. "We'll do some Light simulations aided by computer." She turned over the tablet and began to tap on the screen again. "Let me just try something." She checked the electrodes on Jackson's chest. "I'm going to try to use an electrical current to stimulate the mutated DNA."

"That doesn't sound safe," I argued.

"He won't feel anything," she reassured me. "We'll be able to see how it reacts to the world around us."

Jackson took a deep breath. "Hit me, doc."

Ramona entered some commands on the machine closest to the chair, then turned her calculating gaze back onto her subject.

Suddenly, Jackson jerked, his hands clawing at the armrests. Ramona turned off the current, but it did nothing to stop the convulsions. He was having a seizure that looked a lot like someone in the throes of possession.

"Jackson!" I cried. I sprang forward, but Wilder caught me around the waist.

"Don't touch him, Purples," he warned.

"Do something!" I pleaded.

"I can't." Ramona stood back, watching as my friend convulsed.

Tears prickled in my eyes. "*No…*"

Abruptly, Jackson gasped, his eyes rolled back into his head, before they snapped to attention. "I saw them…" he rasped trying to catch his breath. "Demons and blood." His gaze fixed on mine. "They saw me, Scarlett. *They can see——*"

"Close your eyes," Ramona cried, shutting off the array of machines. "*Now.*"

Jackson did as she commanded, the panic clear on his face.

"What's going on?" I demanded.

"There's a link," she replied, rushing around the

room. "There's no other explanation. He doesn't have any Darkness."

"A link?"

"What Darkness?" Jackson squeaked.

"A link to the demons," Wilder said, looking troubled. "Whatever they did to him has connected them somehow."

"Will someone tell me what Darkness is?" Jackson boomed.

"Magic," I said, placing my hand on his. "Like my Light, greater demons have their own version."

"If he had Darkness…" Wilder trailed off and turned his eyes towards Ramona.

She nodded sharply. "We need to summon the council." She took out her mobile phone and began to type out a text message. It was such an unexpected sight, I blinked at her in surprise.

"If he had Darkness, what?" Jackson demanded, his eyes still firmly closed.

"Yeah, what?" I echoed.

"The contact would be deliberate," Wilder explained.

"I'm not contacting anybody!" my best friend exclaimed. "Like I would ever help them after what they did to me!"

"They made your life a thousand times better," Wilder stated. "You're stronger, your eyesight is twenty-twenty, you can actually pick up women—"

"Wilder!" I punched him in the arm as hard as I could, but he didn't flinch. "If he says he's not helping them, *he's not helping them.*"

"They're on their way," Ramona said. She returned to her station and began to remove the electrodes from Jackson's head. "Better keep your eyes closed for now."

"Ow!" he cried. "That's my hair you're pulling out!"

Jackson could tune into the all access demon channel? This was bad news. A big, bad, hunk of bad news.

It wasn't long before Brax strode into the lab, looking like a thunder cloud personified. He was followed by the much calmer Aldrich, and ever the picture of serenity, Greer floated along behind them.

Ramona explained the situation as they looked on, their expressions changing into various stages of shock and concern.

"This is a disaster," Brax said with a snarl. "You let a spy into the Sanctum."

"I'm not a spy!" Jackson exclaimed, his eyes still closed.

"Not knowingly."

"We have to be calm about this," Aldrich said. "There's a lot to consider."

"More study has to be undertaken," Ramona declared, checking Jackson's temperature. "The vision could just be a premonition."

"I don't know… It felt a lot like live TV," Jackson drawled.

"You're not helping yourself," I hissed at him.

"What did you see?" Greer asked, her angelic voice a note of calmness in a chaotic sea.

He shivered. "A guy putting himself back together with severed body parts. He seemed to sense I was watching. It was kinda perverted."

Glancing at Wilder, I whispered, "The Balan."

If Jackson could contact the Balan demon—the same creature who'd murdered my parents and attacked the Sanctum—then this was bad. Like, *apocalyptic* bad.

"We have to summon the Inquisitor," Brax said. "This is bigger than the London Sanctum now."

I glanced at Wilder. This was the first I'd heard of a hierarchy above the three leaders before me. Here I was thinking Greer was the closest thing to absolute authority with her position as the protector of the Codex.

"We don't know if this link poses any threat," Aldrich countered. "Let Ramona conduct more tests before we get Julius involved. Greer?"

Her brow was knitted together as she studied the readings on the machines.

"I think Brax is correct," she said slowly, though her tone implied she wasn't entirely convinced. "There's no way to be entirely certain this link isn't already being exploited by the demons."

Jackson shifted, his nerves obvious. "But I don't want this," he said. "I'm not passing anything to anyone. Why would I? It'd put Scarlett in danger."

"We're not questioning your intentions, Jackson," Greer said kindly.

"The demons could be using you as a conduit

without your knowledge," Brax said. "That makes you dangerous, willing or not."

Ramona looked troubled as she began to remove the electrodes from Jackson's chest.

"I'll vouch for him," I said, desperate to keep my friend from being locked up, because that's where this was going and *fast*. "What do I need to do?"

"We appreciate your sentiment, Scarlett, but you can't vouch for this," Aldrich said.

"I'm recommending that he's moved to the vaults," Brax stated, his eyes flashing cooly. "We can monitor and isolate him until the Inquisitor can be summoned. In the meantime, Ramona can continue her studies."

I glanced at Wilder, but his expression was closed. He was watching everything that was happening, his gaze flashing to Jackson more than the others. What was he looking for?

"I'm going to be locked up again?" Jackson asked. "No—"

"I'm sorry," Greer said, placing her hand on his arm, "but it's for everyone's safety."

"It's not ideal, but I agree," Aldrich said to Brax. "This affects us all. It would be irresponsible to keep the other Sanctums out of the loop."

"But what will happen to him?" I asked. "If he's being used, then we have to find a way to stop it."

"Don't rush ahead, Scarlett," Greer said. "We'll figure this out, but you have to understand there's a bigger threat here."

"The Sanctum was already infiltrated once,"

Wilder said, speaking for the first time. "If it happens again, we could lose everything."

"Wilder is correct," Brax said, glaring at the Natural, his distaste on display for all to see. "We almost lost Greer and the Codex. This boy is the closest thing you have to family, and he was mutated by a rogue demon. Please put two and two together, Miss Ravenwood. You are a Natural now."

I scowled, the reprimand grating against my ego, and glanced at Jackson, who looked like he was about to puke.

"It's okay, Scarlett," Jackson said. He put on his T-shirt and slipped his arms into his jacket. "It's just a precaution, right?"

"I…" I didn't like it, but it wasn't my call. I had zero say about any of this.

Well, he was right about one thing—I was just a solider in their war, a tool against the Dark.

My hands shook as I watched Aldrich and Brax file out after Jackson and his Natural escort.

"He'll be well-looked after," Greer said, standing beside me. "Until we know how the link works, this is the best course of action."

"I know," I said. "It's just…" I tossed my hands out in defeat.

"I understand," she replied. "Please don't panic unnecessarily." Offering me a smile, she followed the others out of the lab, leaving me and Wilder alone.

"C'mon, Purples," he said, nudging me towards the door, "we've still got a few hours of training."

"I can't focus on training."

He smirked and pushed me a little harder. "That's why I'm going to make you do cardio instead."

There was no escaping him, but there was nothing I could do for Jackson right now. Maybe running on the treadmill would help relieve a little stress.

"Do you really think the demons would try to take me?" I asked as we walked down the hall.

"Try to keep up with the threat level, Purples. We're at D for *Duh*."

"Who is this Inquisitor guy?" I went on, starting to get my ramble on. "It sounds like he enjoys burning demons at the stake."

"Julius Wainthrope, and yes, he's just as pretentious as his name sounds."

I snorted.

"The Inquisitor is there to stop Sanctums from turning into splinter groups and doing whatever they like," he replied irritably. "The Naturals have to be a unified front, otherwise we'd never make any headway with the demon incursion. Wars are fought together, otherwise chaos reigns. This thing with Jackson affects us all."

"Why am I only hearing about this douche now?"

"The London Sanctum has always operated on some level of autonomy because of the Codex," he explained.

"Like a black ops site?"

"I suppose so." He shrugged. "Greer and Aldrich don't tell me what's going on, and Brax especially doesn't let anything slip. All I have is suspicion, and I don't operate on theory, Purples. I like facts."

"And what facts do you know?"

He stopped in his tracks and I almost slammed into him. "Think about it, will you?" he sneered with a scowl.

I rubbed the bridge of my nose. "Ugh, don't tell me this is another one of your teaching moments."

He glowered and I shook my head, clearing away my anxiety over Jackson. I'd asked him to come here and he was being locked up, *again*, but it was about more than his mutation. It always came back to Arondight. The sword was everyone's end game, which didn't just make me a target… *I was the target.*

"No one else knows I'm here, do they?" I asked, dread pooling in my gut.

"Oh, they know about you, but not everything," Wilder replied. "I suspect Greer hasn't told them about your affinity with Arondight."

"Why? Doesn't she trust our own people?"

"It's not all for one and one for all," he shot back. "Not all humans are fighting for the same agenda, are they? It's the same with us, Purples. Life is never that simple."

I'd spent all this time learning how to fight demons and now I had to worry about my own people, too? If this Inquisitor knew about my contact with Arondight, what would he do? Take me away and experiment on me? Use Light to pry my memories from my mind? I'd become a lab rat, just like Jackson. What had I done bringing my best friend back here?

I slapped my palm against my forehead and

groaned in frustration. "I need to see Jackson. I can't leave him again."

I made to walk off, but Wilder grasped my arm.

"Go after dinner," he said. "I know you think you're about to be betrayed, but Greer and Aldrich won't let any undue harm come to him."

"And Brax?" I scowled.

"Brax does things by the book." Which, in my mind, made him dangerous.

"I don't trust him."

"Say that a little louder, Purples," Wilder said, rolling his eyes. "Your probation has barely been lifted and you're already mouthing off your superiors."

"Wait… When was my probation lifted?"

Wilder smirked in that annoyingly handsome and arrogant way he had. "The other day."

"Why didn't you tell me!" I shrieked.

He slapped his hands over his ears. "Because I knew you'd get into trouble five seconds later and have it reinstated in record time."

"This is bad," I murmured, fisting my hands into my hair. "So, so, *bad*."

"Which is why we need to train," Wilder said. "You have to be able to control your Light, Purples."

"What's going to happen to him?" I asked again. "What's going to happen to me?"

Wilder's eyes narrowed. He didn't know the answer, either.

"Then I want to know how to use my Light," I said, my lip curling. "If it comes down to it, I'll—"

"What did I just say about running your mouth

off?" He grasped my upper arm and began to drag me through the Sanctum. "We don't know anything yet, so untwist your knickers."

"If it comes down to it, I'll do what I have to do, you know."

"I know…" he said, "and that's what worries me."

---

I'd calmed down by dinnertime. Wilder let me off my diet for the night, so the lamb casserole, with chocolate mousse and whipped cream for dessert, went a long way to soothing the whirlwind of fury I'd been all afternoon.

When I got to the vaults, I was let in by the guards without any objections.

The floor-to-celling bars, and metallic walls and floors, were unsettlingly familiar. So was the chill in the air. Jackson sat on the ground beside the bed, his arms resting on his drawn-up knees.

"Fancy meeting you here again," he said when he raised his head.

I curled my hands around the bars. "I'm so sorry."

"It's not your fault."

"Feels like it."

He drew in a deep breath, looking exhausted, which was saying something considering he was supposed to be this hybrid super solider.

"I know I was mad at you, Scarlett, but I'd never let them use me to get to you," he said. "I'm not the vindictive type. At least…I think I'm not."

"You're not," I said firmly. "And I believe you."

"I'm sorry how things went between us. I was hurt and I lashed out. I shouldn't have let it get that far."

I shifted from foot to foot. I'd thought about it a lot since the night he left the Sanctum. How I could have been so blind to his feelings for me? I'd been distracted by all the stuff going on with Wilder and discovering the demon world, but before that, I'd been so wrapped up in my own problems I hadn't noticed. If we were talking about guilt, I had plenty of my own.

"Don't worry about it."

"I know I'm a part of this now," Jackson went on. "There's no escaping your war anymore."

"I screwed up again," I wailed. "I thought I was doing the right thing by bringing you back. Ramona said—"

"You better not tell me anything," he interrupted. "Nothing about your training, the whole purple thing, what the Naturals are up to. On second thoughts, it's probably better not to talk to me at all."

I curled my hands around the bars. "Jackson, I can't just leave you here."

"If this is a two-way street, then they're already listening. Who knows how long they've been in my head? I'm not going to do anything that puts your life in danger, Scarlett."

"They mightn't know yet," I argued.

"I agree with Greer and her man posse. I don't want to take that chance."

"Even if they try to cut you open?"

He lowered his gaze and swallowed hard. "Don't remind me."

"If you could help…would you?"

He shrugged. "Do I have a choice?"

"Of course you have a choice," I replied.

He was silent for so long, I was starting to believe he wasn't going to reply. Then, he met my gaze and said, "Who am I to pass up a chance to save the world? A video game is one thing, but to do it for real?"

*I knew he'd say yes.* Jackson was pure, and no demon mutation could ever change that. I smiled, but a part of me was on the verge of bursting into a flood of tears.

I wanted to tell him that everything would be okay, but I couldn't promise him something I couldn't deliver. He'd had his life irrevocably changed because of who I was. Before this was over—if it ever reached that point—more people would get hurt. Romy, Greer, Alo, Valeria, Martin, Aldrich…*Wilder*. No one was safe anymore.

And it was all because of Arondight.

## 7

It was so quiet, I imagined I could hear a pin drop on the other side of the Sanctum.

Everyone who wasn't on duty had assembled in the foyer, our stoic figures overseen by the massive statue of the Lady of the Lake. It was formal and a little terrifying, if I was being honest with myself, almost like we were waiting for a storm to strike us down.

Wilder was beside me, and Romy was on my other side, our hands clasped behind our backs as we stood to attention. Greer, Aldrich, and Brax waited at the head of our ranks, their gazes locked on the entrance.

There'd been a heaviness in the air ever since it was announced that the Inquisitor was coming. It didn't take me long to realise it wasn't an honour to host such a high ranking Natural, but an irritation. We enjoyed far too many freedoms, and everyone knew it.

Training with Wilder was one thing, but now my

position as a Natural was becoming as real as a human solider poised on the front lines of a battlefield, gun in hand. I was part of the hierarchy, but I was at the bottom of the barrel.

The doors flew open, the sound echoing off the walls and bouncing around the glass dome. A wave of unfamiliar Naturals strode into the Sanctum, their boots thumping across the marble. At their head was a tall man with long blonde hair, a chiselled expression, and hard grey eyes. I had to lean a little to the side to get a good look at him, but there was no doubt this guy was the dreaded Inquisitor, Julius Wainthrope.

He walked with all the air and grace of a dictator and dressed like a flamboyant goth—he had a long, black trench coat on over a crimson collared shirt, black trousers, and matching winkle-picker shoes. He'd fit right in at a goth club in Camden, that's for sure. He even had that cliquey aloofness down pat.

The Inquisitor came to a halt in the centre of the foyer and raked his gaze over the assembly. Whatever he thought about us, he didn't show in his expression as his entourage of black-clad Naturals lined up in formation behind him.

"Inquisitor Wainthrope," Greer said, inclining her head in a gesture of respect, "welcome to the London Sanctum."

"Spare your pleasantries, Greer," he said, his gaze cool. "This isn't a diplomatic visit. It's an inquiry."

From the look on her face, Greer was not

expecting that the Inquisitor was here to do a stocktake of the Sanctum's comings and goings.

"After the breach, I would have expected you to be more forthcoming," he said without even so much as a blink. It gave him an evil appearance and I instantly bristled. "I have to wonder what else you have left out of your reports."

*Remain calm, Scarlett.*

His gaze raked over the assembled Naturals, and I resisted the urge to hide behind the guy in front of me. The Inquisitor's eyes seemed to fix on me for half a second longer than everyone else before he moved on, but I couldn't be sure.

Whatever his assessment of the London Sanctum was, I didn't know. His expression didn't change once. Not even his eyeballs twitched. All he did was turn and stride into the main hallway like he owned us all. And I suppose he did in a way.

The moment he glided from the foyer, followed by the council and the unfamiliar Natural escort, we all sighed in relief and broke rank.

"That was tense," I drawled.

"It will be until he leaves," Romy declared. "Better be on your best behaviour."

"My reputation proceeds me." I mock bowed, much to Wilder's annoyance.

"Best not advertise, Purples," he said, raising an eyebrow.

"So I don't get to practice with my arondight blade?" Disappointment flared inside me and I pouted. I know I complained, but I was really starting to find my love of fighting. It gave me the strength I'd longed for my entire life.

"Wilder's got a point," Romy said, patting me on the shoulder. She waved to us as she returned to her duties, leaving Wilder and I alone in the foyer.

Everyone else had cleared out, wanting nothing more than to get away from the tense energy left behind by the high and mighty Inquisitor.

"C'mon," Wilder said, "it's no use hanging around here."

We returned to the gym where several groups of Naturals were discussing the hot topic of the day—Jackson and the incoming Inquisition.

"He's going to get fried," some guy said. "Wainthrope is going to pry him open with his Light."

"It's not his fault," a woman replied. "He can't help what happened to him."

"It's not about fault. That guy was mutated by a demon. We all know they have a single purpose."

"Don't listen to them," Wilder said, noticing my building rage. "They don't know the whole story." I took a step towards them, but his hand shot out, grabbing my upper arm. "Leave it, Scarlett."

Seeing red, I shook him off. Approaching the group of Naturals, I tapped the guy—the one with the big mouth—on the shoulder. He turned and stared at me, his eyebrows rising.

"Excuse me," I drawled, "you want to shut your mouth up about my best friend?"

"Well, if it isn't Miss Demon Lover herself," he replied with a smirk.

A flare of pure rage flared inside me and I felt my Light tingle. Shoving it away before I lost control, I glared at him, wondering how Wilder controlled himself under the onslaught of such ignorance. Unlucky for the Natural standing in front of me, I didn't have a shred of the control my mentor held.

"You have no idea…" I snarled. "None at all. So you better shut your mouth before your lies come back and bite you in the arse."

He laughed and sized me up. "And what are you going to do to stop me? A *woman* your size?"

I didn't like the way he said the word woman and I bristled. "Let's spar," I declared. "If I win, you shut the hell up about Jackson and learn your manners."

"And if I win, I get a kiss. *Full tongue.*"

I scowled and grabbed a practice staff from the rack. *Pervert.* "Is that all?" I taunted. "You can't do better than a kiss?"

"I can." The Natural's gaze darkened. "You'll see."

"Staffs, no Light," I said. "I want to beat you on skill alone."

He grinned, under the impression I'd just handed him the win. "You're on."

Wilder grasped my shoulder and turned me around. "You do realise I can order you to stand down."

"But I know you won't," I fired back. "How many fights did you get into at the academy protecting your honour?" He narrowed his eyes and I snorted. "See?"

"That guy has a good ten years of experience on you, Purples. You can't win."

"*Says you.*"

"If you lose, he won't just go after a kiss," Wilder said angrily. "He'll press you for more, even if you say *no*."

"All the more reason to teach him a lesson."

It took him a moment, but Wilder seemed to realise there was no stopping me. "Don't use your Light, not even by accident."

"I know."

"Purples…" He gave me a look that had concern etched into it and I felt a pang ricochet in my heart.

"I can't believe you're endorsing this," I declared, taking the piss, rather than give into the feelings I could allow myself to have.

"You know I'm not endorsing anything."

"If I lose, I'll make sure he *only* gets his kiss."

Wilder's gaze darkened. "Don't lose, Purples."

My fingers began to ache like they did when I desperately wanted to touch something I couldn't and I tightened them around the staff.

Stepping past him, I pushed away the unfamiliar feelings and kicked off my boots. The mat was cool against my bare feet and I stretched, waiting for my opponent to do the same. The fact that this was my first fight with a Natural other than Wilder hadn't escaped me, but there was no way I was backing out now. Besides, I had to learn sometime, right?

Facing off against the Natural, I centred myself just like Wilder had taught me. There was a reason I picked the staff—as my second favourite weapon next to my arondight blade, I was constantly drilling with it.

The guy sneered arrogantly, already believing he had this in the bag. Seriously, how could a woman who'd only been training seven weeks take him out? *Well, he was about to find out.*

We clashed, the force of the blow vibrating up my arms. I was pushed back, stumbling a few steps before I regained my balance and dodged to the side as another strike came my way. I twisted, my staff following my movement, and I brought down the end on his lower back, then struck at his knee with my heel.

My foot slammed into the Natural right where I wanted it, and he crumpled to the mat. He rolled, sweeping his staff at my legs.

I fell, my back hitting the mat and the air drove from my lungs. Wilder had taught me how to continue fighting if I was winded, and I immediately sucked in a deep breath as I rolled to the side, narrowly avoiding a staff to the face.

"Hey!" Wilder shouted from the sidelines, but the Natural wasn't listening.

He struck again, but I'd kept moving clear across the mat. I used the momentum to push to my feet and sweep the heel of my staff around. The Natural hadn't anticipated the move and the staff slammed into the side of his head, sending his bulky frame reeling.

A tense moment passed as I stared down at his

prone body, then the assembled Naturals began to hoot and holler. *I'd knocked the guy out cold!*

My chest heaved and I relaxed out of my fighting stance, putting a few steps between me and my opponent.

Abruptly, the gym fell deathly silent and I felt the cold presence of authority lingering behind me. *Uh oh…*

Turning, I saw the Inquisitor watching us with interest, flanked by the council. Greer looked troubled, Brax was impassive as usual, and Aldrich seemed impressed…to a degree.

Julius Wainthrope smiled the way a serial killer smiled over his prey, and I suppressed a shudder of revulsion.

"Impressive," he said, his creepy smile widening. "And you are?"

I set the staff on the floor, never taking my gaze off him. "Scarlett Ravenwood, sir."

He studied every inch of me, before he said, "Keep up the good work, Miss Ravenwood."

No one moved until the entourage left the gym, and when they did, voices began to murmur excitedly. Wilder didn't look impressed, and I felt a pang of regret…and disappointment.

The Natural who I'd just beaten to a pulp spat and glared up at me. He'd regained consciousness just in time to find out he'd just been humiliated in front of one of the most powerful men in the Naturals' hierarchy.

"Need a hand?" I asked sweetly. "You can use your right one to get—"

"*Scarlett,*" Wilder barked.

I walked away, not feeling any better about protecting Jackson's reputation. I'd just made an enemy *and* drawn attention to myself.

*Nice going, Scarlett.* I'd just done the next best thing to running headfirst into danger as I could get.

---

When dinnertime rolled around, I was relieved to leave the gym, my fight, and my encounter with the Inquisitor behind.

Romy, Martin, Valeria, and Alo were sitting at our usual table, and once I'd collected my meal, I joined them.

They were eyeing the group of Naturals who'd escorted the Inquisitor when I sat down.

"You do realise they know you're staring them," I said, sprinkling a little salt onto my asparagus stalks. It didn't make them taste any more deliciously bland, but it was better than nothing.

"Everyone's staring," Romy declared. "We aren't special."

"They're mean looking," Valeria said.

"They'd have to be to be chosen as the Inquisitor's personal guard," Alo chimed in.

Martin rolled his eyes, but I caught the envious glance he threw them directly after.

"What do you know about the guy?" I asked.

Wilder hadn't been forthcoming in our training that afternoon, and his attempts at distracting me hadn't quietened my anxiety over Jackson one bit. He did, however, explain the Natural hierarchy to me since we'd skipped it in favour of combat training and demonology.

Each Sanctum had their ruling council of three—London was extra special because of the Codex, which made it one of the ruling Sanctums, similar to the human concept of a capital city. An independent board of notable Naturals tied all these sites together, known as the Regula—Latin for rule. They existed to ensure the Naturals remained one cohesive force against the Darkness—and to keep any rogue operations in check.

The Inquisitor was the Natural who was chosen to lead this elite group and keep the law, and that made Julius an extremely powerful man.

"He's the youngest Inquisitor since the fall of Camelot," Romy replied. "Not much of a warrior, but apparently he's calculating—"

"And cold," Valeria interrupted. "Real nasty if you get on his bad side."

"He takes his job seriously," Martin added. "The law is the law, no matter what."

I stabbed a stalk of asparagus with my fork. Jackson, the nicest, purest, self-sacrificing guy I knew, was on his bad side.

"Poor Jackson," Romy said with a sigh.

"I know." I desperately wanted to see Jackson, but he was right. I didn't want him to be, but he could have an active link to the Balan demon that murdered my parents and was after me. If he was unknowingly giving away information, then he'd never forgive himself.

"What do you think will happen?" Valeria asked.

"He'll review the evidence and make a ruling," Martin said matter-of-factly.

"Do you think he'll make a move against Greer?" Alo mused.

"He wouldn't dare," Romy replied. "She's the protector of the Codex. It won't let just anyone read it, let alone touch it."

"I heard he watched you train today," Valeria said to me. "You kicked Thompson's arse."

"Thompson?" Romy asked, her eyes widening. "Seriously?"

"What's so special about him?" I grumbled. I hadn't even known his name and he was acting on rumour. "He was trash talking my best friend. I beat him fair and square."

"You're not winning yourself any friends," Martin said. "You bruised his ego and he'll want payback."

I rolled my eyes. "*Whatever.*"

"We all know about your affinity, Scarlett," Romy said. "If he wants to, Thompson could out you to the Inquisitor."

I was such a moron. "Then why doesn't he? Why hasn't anyone?"

"We've been ordered not to," Alo explained, "by Greer herself."

Their trust in the protector of the Codex wasn't

lost on me. It was also a nod to how loyal the London Naturals were to their leader and their shared cause. If Greer said jump, I was sure everyone would ask how high.

She'd asked them to protect my affinity with Arondight, but it wouldn't be long before word spread. Soon, I'd be on everyone's most-wanted list. The danger rating on the Inquisitor just kept rising, along with my fear of what he could do to Jackson.

"Why didn't I know about the order?" I asked.

Alo shrugged. "I assume Wilder would have ordered you to keep yourself under the radar."

I shook my head. "Not in so many words." He wasn't one for direct orders, which was infuriating at the best of times. Sometimes I wished he would say what he meant, rather than try to teach me lessons in conjecture.

"Well, let's put it this way... Who would you rather be controlled by?" Valeria asked. "Greer or Julius?"

"Point taken."

"We've got your back, Scarlett," Romy said with a bright smile. "Just try to keep out of trouble, okay?"

I glowered, the shine from my win rubbing right off. "It's a mean feat, but I'll give it a crack."

8

---

A general assembly was called the very next morning.

I was walking out of the kitchen, following the stream of Naturals, when Wilder accosted me in the hall. He looked surlier than usual, and my heartbeat sped up.

"Greer ripped me a new arsehole for what happened yesterday," he said. "Thanks for that."

"You're welcome."

"Thompson may have deserved to be taken down a few pegs, but not in front of Wainthrope."

"How come everyone know his name and I don't?" I glowered.

"Check your arrogance and hot head at the door, Purples. There's a time and a place to kick a mouthy arsehole's arse."

"Yeah? When's that? Are you looking for a place in line?"

He raised his eyebrows. "Well, it's not in front of the entire Sanctum, the council, and the Inquisitor."

I groaned and glanced at a group of Naturals who were throwing me curious glances. It'd become obvious that no one had thought I was going to be as good as I was, let alone win against a more experienced fighter. Honestly, I was just as surprised as they were.

Romy was right about one thing—eventually, things stopped hurting…and began to make sense.

"Don't beat yourself up about it, Purples," Wilder drawled. "We've got bigger fish to fry today."

"Why is everyone going to this thing anyway?" I asked as we climbed the stairs. "I thought this would be something between leaders."

"Wainthrope wants to make an example out of us," he replied. "Or he's already made up his mind and wants to cut down the chain of command in front of everyone to make a point."

I made a face. "He sounds like a bully to me."

"He is."

"What do you think will happen to Jackson?"

"Nothing good."

I opened my mouth to ask another question, but Romy and Martin appeared next to us, and I clamped it shut.

"You two are basically glued at the hip!" Romy declared. "It's cute."

I pretended to puke while Wilder flat-out ignored her.

"That's because she's his only friend," Martin

said. "Only because she was ordered to train with him."

"Martin!" Romy scowled at him.

"Isn't that like you and Romy?" I asked. "If you weren't assigned as partners, I'm not sure your attitude would win you any friends. You're lucky to have her."

"Ooh! Burn!" She began to laugh as I threaded my arm through Wilder's and guided him away.

I could feel him tense as we moved through the assembling Naturals, my grip on him unfamiliar.

"You can say it, you know," I said, ignoring the rising heat in my body.

"Say what?" he asked, his jaw tense.

"That you hate Martin with the fire of a million trillion suns."

"I don't hate him. I hate his prejudice. There's a difference."

"How?"

"He was brought up in a society that taught him certain beliefs," he clipped. It was also a tone that meant his opinion was final and there was no chance of further discussion.

Sometimes I disliked the finality he saw things with. He'd already made up his mind about the world and saw no chance for change. I knew he'd been through a lot and was constantly reminded of his differences, but his lack of hope for redemption was bruising everyone around him.

"Wilder—"

"Not now, Purples."

We entered the auditorium, which was coincidentally where I'd had my Light test when I'd first arrived at the Sanctum. It seemed so long ago now, but the time and the familiarity didn't take the edge off the cold, intimidating room.

Bench seating ringed around the entire space in four tiers and in the centre, I spied a clearing with a scary chair complete with arm and leg restraints. Before what I was calling the 'operating armchair', sat a long table with five seats. No doubt that's where the council, the Inquisitor, and his chosen yes-man would sit.

Wilder chose a space towards the back where we'd be hidden and give us a good view of the other members of the London Sanctum. Across the theatre, Thompson glared at me and I rolled my eyes before focusing elsewhere.

Romy and Martin sat a row down, and Alo and Valeria were towards the front to our left. I recognised a lot of faces around us, but I was still at a loss matching names to those faces. There were almost eighty Naturals in residence, including the council, so it'd take time to get to know everyone. Training twelve hours a day, seven days a week, didn't leave much time for socialising.

When the council walked in, we all rose as a mark of respect. The Inquisitor followed, making a show of flipping his jacket and arranging himself in the centre position of the table. When he was done, he produced his arondight blade and sat the hilt before him.

I couldn't see the detailing from where we were

sitting, but it didn't take much squinting to realise it was jewel-encrusted.

*What a pompous twit.* I snorted, earning myself a sharp elbow in my side from Wilder.

Wainthrope's second-in-command sat beside him —a middle-aged man with a hard, weathered look about him—and placed a pile of bound papers on the table. Greer sat on the Inquisitor's right, then Aldrich beside her. On the opposite end of the table, Brax took his place next to the unknown advisor. The split was telling and my growing distrust for Brax began to gain mass.

Once they were settled, we took our sets and waited for the assembly to begin.

Not wasting any time, Julius Wainthrope stood and walked the length of the table, his fingertips gliding across the surface. The room was in complete silence as he moved, his footsteps echoing off the walls.

"Welcome, fellow Naturals," he said, his voice booming through the auditorium. "It's an honour to be hosted within the walls of your esteemed Sanctum. I was fortunate enough to lay eyes on the Codex and what a sight it was, but today we have more important matters to discuss. A new danger has emerged, threatening the delicate balance between Light and Dark." I knew this was coming, but I tensed anyway. "We are here to discuss the mutated human currently being held in the vaults under our very feet. It is not something to be whispered about behind closed doors, but with everyone within these walls. It affects you all *and* the greater world."

"Jackson is not a threat," Greer said. "He has been one hundred percent cooperative."

"He's immune to alteration," Wainthrope exclaimed. "And his physical form has been altered. He's basically a demonic super solider. Releasing him is out of the question. And who knows what secrets he's giving away to the enemy."

"But his intent—"

"I don't care about his intent." His voice dripped with venom. "We can't even tell if he's lying. A demon will never tell the truth, you know that."

"I stopped the mutation," Ramona said, rising from her seat in the front row. "I'm confident the subject is in full control of his mind."

"And his soul?" The Inquisitor raised his eyebrows, clearly not pleased with being challenged by someone of lower rank. "The mutation has changed him on a fundamental level. It's right here in your research, doctor." He flipped through the report on the table in front of him. "*The growth in the subject's chest appears to be demonic in nature and serves as an engine for the mutation,*" he quoted. "Do you deny it? This is your report, correct?"

"It is my report, sir."

"Then you will know that his soul bears no resemblance to the one he left here with six weeks ago."

I stifled a gasp and grabbed Wilder's arm. "What

are they talking about?" I whispered into his ear. "What's wrong with Jackson's soul?"

Wilder shook his head. Apparently, he didn't know, either.

Wainthrope turned to face the table. "And tell me, esteemed council, did the subject make contact with the same Balan demon who breached this very Sanctum, or did he not?"

The council was lost for words, their silence confirming the Inquisitor's statement.

"He did." He smirked and swept his arm wide. "All while he was within these very walls!"

The assembled Naturals began to murmur amongst themselves. Brax rose to his feet and slammed his fist on the tabletop, bringing everyone back to attention, but the damage was already done.

"Something must be done," Wainthrope declared. "That is a must, but what?"

Ramona rose to her feet again. "If I may, Inquisitor?"

"Yes, Ramona? Do you have a suggestion?"

"More research. If—"

"More research?" he scoffed. "Research is useless when action is needed. This threat exists *now*. The demons won't wait until you've drawn your conclusions, doctor."

"Then what do you propose, Inquisitor Wainthrope?" Greer asked, her tone icy. I'd never heard her speak with so much disdain for another Natural in my life—not even when she was reprimanding me or Wilder.

"This is not a dictatorship," Wainthrope said, his gaze raking over the room. "This does not come down to one man's assessment. Each one of you will get a say in the matter."

"A vote?" Aldrich asked.

"Yes, a vote," the Inquisitor replied. "Now you've heard the facts, you can all make an informed decision."

I ground my teeth together. His 'facts' were manipulative truths twisted into scary stories designed to get his way. If you asked me, it was a dictatorship in all but name.

I glanced at Wilder, who motioned for me to keep my mouth shut.

"I propose the Sanctum casts their votes at midday tomorrow," the Inquisitor addressed the assembly.

"Tomorrow?" Greer asked. "A day doesn't give enough time to form a fair and just opinion."

He turned on her, folding his hands behind his back. "Given the evidence presented here today, I feel it is more than adequate."

"There has been no trial. A vote can't be held unless all parties have had their chance to speak."

Wainthrope raised an eyebrow. "You would have the demon present a case for itself?"

"He is more human than demon," Greer challenged.

The Inquisitor stood tall, asserting his authority. "Are you forgetting what the Codex teaches, Greer?"

"I am the protector," she declared. "I don't forget anything."

"Then tell me, *protector*, what was the doctrine set down by the Naturals in the wake of the cataclysm?"

I tensed, remembering the story from my studies. The Naturals losses had been so great in the fall of Camelot that a zero-tolerance policy had been adopted. Demons had no soul, were ruthless, and would not yield, *no matter what*. There would be no bargaining, no mercy, and no hesitation. That's why the council had made a big deal over my answers when I'd come to the Sanctum wanting to be one of them.

But those laws had been made a thousand years ago. The world had changed, but I knew Wainthrope didn't care—he wanted Jackson to burn.

Greer squirmed and I bit my bottom lip. The Inquisitor had her, and she knew it.

"The eyes have it," he said, leaning slightly towards the table. He then turned to the assembly. "Take the rest of the day to discuss and think upon your decision, but…" he paused, making sure no one had moved, "before we close the proceedings for the day, I'd like to discuss another serious matter."

"It's becoming late, Inquisitor," Greer said, her voice weary. "Perhaps we can bring up this item as our first topic prior to the vote?"

"This cannot wait." He shot a withering glare at Greer. "Your new recruit is intimately acquainted with the subject."

"I'm not intimately acquainted," I hissed under my breath. Wilder grasped my knee and I tensed.

"The recruit is in her late twenties, never knew she manifested, and has shown accelerated abilities during her preliminary training," Wainthrope went on. "Why mutate him of all humans?"

"Coincidence," Aldrich said. "A new recruit could easily be tricked, but Scarlett is a special case. She's not a child at the academy."

The Inquisitor *harrumphed*. "Because they knew you'd save him."

"We'd save anyone who was threatened by a demon," Greer said. "The Codex demands it."

"And do you think her choosing that blade was pure coincidence?" he asked. "I think not."

"What are they talking about?" I hissed at Wilder.

His eyes narrowed and I noticed he was grinding his teeth.

"Don't trust him," he whispered. "Greer and the others will protect you, but——"

"*Scarlett Ravenwood.*"

I tensed as the Inquisitor's voice boomed through the assembly.

My heart leapt as all eyes turned towards me. I was frozen, panic fixing my arse to the bench.

"Miss Ravenwood," the Inquisitor boomed, "please approach the council." He gestured to the scary interrogation-slash-torture chair in the centre of the assembly.

Wilder nudged me and I shot to my feet, swallowing the hard lump in my throat. My footsteps echoed as I descended the stairs, my anxiety rising the closer I came to the Inquisitor. Everyone was staring, their eyeballs burning holes in my back, my sides, my front. I was circled by my peers, but I was facing my enemy.

Was he my enemy, though? He was supposed to be on my side, but I knew I'd be at his mercy if he found out about my contact with Arondight.

I sat on the chair, the leather creaking loudly in the silence. I curled my hands around the armrests, my mouth suddenly dryer than the Sahara.

"Miss Ravenwood," Wainthrope said, smiling down at me, "welcome."

I nodded, my tongue tied into knots.

"I understand you've excelled in your training," he went on, returning to his seat behind the table. "How long have you been under Wilder's tutelage?"

"Seven weeks, your…uh, *sir*." *Oh my God, I was about to call him your excellency*. My cheeks flushed.

"And your arondight blade? Did you choose it for aesthetics, or did it choose you?"

"It chose me, I suppose. I didn't pick it out myself. I was drawn to it."

Julius leaned back and studied me intently. "Do you like the colour purple, Miss Ravenwood?"

I shot him a confused look. "The movie, sir? I can't say that I've seen it." A few sniggers echoed softly around the room.

"*Your hair*, Miss Ravenwood. Your training has covered our history, has it not?"

"Yes, sir, it has." I swallowed hard. "It's Manic Panic."

His eyebrows rose. "Excuse me?"

"It's a brand of hair dye. I've been this colour for so long it's kind of my trademark." He was still staring at me, so I added, "Punk rock." Then I threw in some rock horns in for good measure.

It was all I could do to not to raise his suspicion. If the Inquisitor found out my Light had been tinted by the Indigo Flame, I'd be locked in a cell next to Jackson's. The Naturals were supposed to be on my side, but for the first time, I was afraid of what they could do to me in their desperation to find Arondight.

The London Sanctum was on my wavelength, and Greer would fight for me as protector of the Codex, but even she answered to higher powers.

Wainthrope was obviously irritated by me, which either could be a good thing or a bad. It could raise his interest or force him to dismiss me as an idiot kid. I didn't want to be the latter, but if it'd get him off my case…as long as no one in the Sanctum decided to out me. Brax might, but so far, he'd been silent on the matter.

"How did you not know you possessed Light?" Wainthrope asked, moving the interrogation on. "Manifestation can be a traumatic experience for some, especially if caught unawares."

"My Light was subdued by medication," I replied. "I grew up an orphan and I was diagnosed as having a mental illness. I suppose that stopped me experiencing my manifestation. Until I was brought to the Sanctum, I had no knowledge of demons or that I was a Natural," I swallowed hard, "sir."

"*Humans*," he muttered with apparent disdain. "And what have you discovered about your parents?"

"Nothing to identify them," I replied, which was the truth. "I have very few memories, and those I do have are just fleeting glimpses."

"Tell me," he commanded.

"I, uh…" My hands began to tremble. "My mother's perfume. The colour of her hair—which was dark brown. The feeling I had when she hugged me."

"And your father?"

I lowered my gaze. "Only that he was strong."

"Is that all?" He sounded irritated.

"She was barely a child," Greer said. "Memories are hazy and fleeting in such a young mind."

The room fell silent, the assembly stared at me as I sat on full display. *The Natural touched by Arondight. The secret that must be kept, lest the Sanctum fall.*

Greer and the others knew I wasn't a weapon or a tool to be manipulated, but a capable warrior and ally. It was clear Julius Wainthrope did not share their opinion.

"You will be one to watch, Miss Ravenwood," he declared, rising gracefully. "And I will be watching your progress with much interest." *Great.* "This assembly is dismissed. We will reconvene tomorrow for the vote."

He swept from the theatre, his second-in-command on his heels. The council followed, Greer and Aldrich shooting me concerned glances.

They didn't have to tell me what they were afraid of. Deep down, under all the smart-arse comebacks, I knew.

Tomorrow, Jackson was going to die, then the heat would turn on me.

**9**

---

The entire Sanctum was in an uproar as we left the assembly.

Naturals turned to watch me with curious expressions, the revelations about Jackson and me a hot topic. Beating Thompson's arse yesterday had ruffled feathers and made them realise that the new girl actually had some skills. Fat lot of good it did me. I was in this up to my eyeballs.

Jackson's life was hanging in the balance and I was the centre of the Inquisitor's unwanted attention. It didn't matter how good a fighter I was, this was all about politics. It wasn't that different from human bickering at the Houses of Parliament if you asked me. Just add a few demons and magical superhuman into the pot and the recipe was complete.

"We can't let it happen," I seethed, tugging on Wilder's arm. "We have to do something."

"We?" he asked with a snort. "You're always implying we're a unit, Purples."

"Aren't we?" I demanded.

"Teacher, student." He narrowed his eyes in warning. "We're not partners."

Now he wanted to argue? He was training me on Greer's orders, but we were good together. We flowed on the same wavelength, even if we fought like cats and dogs. We helped one another. Out of all the people in the Sanctum, I trusted him the most.

I stared him down and stated, "*We should be.*"

He shook his head and grabbed my arm, practically dragging me out of the theatre of horrors and back to my room. We passed groups of concerned Naturals, their gazes following us down the hall. His fingers bit into my skin, but I didn't complain; instead, I allowed him to lead me.

It felt strange having Wilder in my room again. He hadn't been here since the night he'd kissed me two months ago. Had it really been that long? It felt like an eternity had passed.

He slammed the door closed and glared at me, trying to force my gaze to the floor, but I refused. Staring at him, I waited for his pearl of wisdom. It had to be something good because he'd been grinding his gears ever since I'd been called up for interrogation.

"I don't even know where to start," he seethed.

"Then don't!" I exclaimed.

"Thompson will out you," he stated. "You made sure of that."

"How was I supposed to know? I was trying to

stick up for my friend. You're supposed to stand up to bullies!"

"This isn't a school playground, Purples," he snarled. "This is life and death for all of us. For the bloody world, if you haven't forgotten."

"Oh, I haven't forgotten! People keep reminding me every hour of every day since I got here!"

"*Then act like it.*"

"Me? Why won't you stand up and do something?" I demanded. "Is it because you'll have to be a part of something? Sad you'll have to give up your loner ways and answer to a higher power? Afraid of a little responsibility?"

"And what do you know about responsibility?" he demanded, closing the distance between us.

He was all up in my personal space as mad as a bee in a jar. The vein in his forehead was pulsing so fast, I was afraid it was going to burst. He was at breaking point, but so was I.

"I understand more than you know," I seethed. "I get how important Arondight is and what that means for me. The night I saw you kill that demon…that happened for a reason, Wilder. You and I met *for a reason.*"

Wilder turned, breaking our death-match staring contest. He paced the length of my room, raking his hands through his hair.

"You're asking a metric shite load of me," he said after a few laps. "You want me to turn against our people, Scarlett. My position here is tenuous as it is.

One misstep—" He broke off and spat out the nastiest word in the English language.

He'd be a wanted criminal, but so would I. Breaking out a human demon-hybrid from prison—one that would be sentenced to death, no doubt—would do that.

"I know it's a lot, Wilder, but think about it. Jackson could lead us to the Balan demon," I argued. "And he could do a lot more than that. If Ramona's right about his abilities and he can control them, we could hit them where it hurts. Tip the balance in our favour until we can find Arondight."

Wilder shook his head, clearly not convinced. "Provided he wants to help."

"*He does.*"

"And I suppose he told you that himself."

"*He did.*"

Wilder turned, picking up the troll doll from my bedside table. He ran his hand over the purple hair, smoothing it into a point. He'd given it to me as an insult back when we'd first met and placed a magical hook on it that'd lead me back to him in case his alteration failed a third time. Ultimately it had, so I'd followed the spell, much to his annoyance. For some reason, I still kept the stupid toy despite his infuriating arrogance. *He'd said it reminded him of me.*

I cared about Wilder, but I'd never admit it to him. I barely admitted it to myself most days.

"You kept it," he murmured.

I shrugged. "It looks like me. I figured it's my mascot."

His lips quirked as he set the toy down.

"The vote means shite," he declared. "But I figured you already understood that."

I nodded. "They'll kill him, Wilder. Wainthrope will pretend it was a democratic vote to cover his own arse, then—"

"Regardless, you're the bigger prize, Purples. Executing Jackson will solidify his power, but you will secure how history remembers him."

*We have to leave.* The realisation slammed into me and I sat on the bed before I fell to my knees. I'd been running my entire life—from foster homes, from my mental illness, from broken hearts, and constant failures—and the thought of repeating all my past mistakes made me feel sick.

The Sanctum had become my home and the Naturals my people, but I wasn't safe here anymore. Jackson wasn't safe, and neither was Wilder.

"You knew it'd come to this, didn't you?" I whispered, my throat tight with rising panic.

"Not until Brax demanded the Inquisitor be called." He knelt in front of me and I focused on his messy hair. "You're not safe here anymore, Scarlett." His eyes glinted silver, and for what felt like the first time, I saw worry in them.

A sharp knock at the door pulled us apart and I wiped at the tears I didn't know were clouding my eyes. Wilder nodded and I called out, "Yeah?"

The door creaked open, revealing Greer's angelic face.

"There you are," she said glancing between us. "Am I interrupting?"

"No," I said hurriedly, "not at all."

Wilder rose to his feet and motioned for her to come in. She closed the door behind her, making sure it was locked this time.

"I gather from the looks on your faces, you understand the situation we find ourselves in," she murmured.

I nodded, not trusting myself to speak.

"We have to get Scarlett out of the Sanctum," Wilder said, "as soon as possible."

"I agree, which is why I'm here. Aldrich is waiting for us in the conservatory. The Codex will protect us."

"Go," Wilder said. "We'll be right behind you."

"You can't tell anyone," she said, looking at me. "At all."

I thought about Romy, Valeria, Alo, and Martin— the closest thing I'd ever had to a posse of best friends —and almost cracked under the weight. *I was doing this for the greater good.*

"You have to act like nothing is amiss," she went on. "You're a Natural, Scarlett, and you must be impartial. Jackson is your friend, but he's also part demon. Do you understand?"

I nodded. I didn't have to agree with it, but I had to play a certain role until we could be smuggled out.

Once Greer had left, Wilder looked around my room. "You don't have much stuff."

"I never had many things," I said. "Stuff weighs you down."

"Have you got your arondight blade?"

I opened my leather jacket and showed him the end of the hilt sicking out of the inside pocket. "Have you got yours?"

"Always," he said with a smirk.

I blew through my lips. "If that's a reference to your penis, I don't want to know about it."

"Well, at least you're still making jokes, Purples." He was back to using my pet name and the mood lightened significantly. "We mightn't get a chance to come back. Is there anything you want to take?"

I glanced at the troll doll. "Is there anything *you* can't bear to leave behind?"

"Better not leave yourself," he stated, nodding at the ugly plastic doll.

I grinned and snatched it up, sliding it into my jacket pocket.

Leaving my room behind, we walked through the Sanctum, acutely aware of the tension in the air. Even with the amount of Naturals housed in this enormous building, the halls were always a little empty, but everyone seemed to have shirked their duties for the evening. Except for those out on patrol, that was.

Every group we passed kept their heads down. The only Naturals that looked comfortable with how things were playing out was the detail the Inquisitor had bought along with him—his merry band of yes-men.

We rounded the corner and took the stairs up to the fourth floor. Once we set foot on the fancy carpet, I turned, only to find our path blocked.

I tensed as I came face to face with Julius Wainthrope, the last man on Earth we wanted to see. Considering we were on a way to a secret meeting to discuss the best way to thwart his super sneaky election tampering, *the timing was wonderful.*

"Miss Ravenwood. Mr…?" He narrowed his eyes at Wilder, who glowered back.

"Wilder," he said.

"Mr. Wilder," Wainthrope drawled.

"Inquisitor," I said with a nod.

"Are you on your way to the conservatory?" he asked, knowing full well there was no other reason for us to be on this level of the Sanctum.

"Greer has granted me some time to look upon the Codex," I replied, the lie slipping from me unbidden.

"She has?" He tilted his head to the side. "That's a rare honour indeed."

"I asked if it was possible after my friend's arrival," I lied, the words rolling off my tongue so smoothly, I even surprised myself. "As I'm still learning the ways of the Naturals, I hoped the Codex would be able to guide me in this troubled time. Greer was kind enough to grant me a slot in her busy schedule."

"And that time is today." His tone relayed the hidden undercurrent of his words as *how convenient.*

"Do you believe in omens, Inquisitor?"

He nodded. "They can be extremely powerful guides if you learn to see beyond the pale."

"Well, I believe this is one of those times.

Whatever I learn here will be important. *I hope.*" I grinned.

Wainthrope looked slightly impressed, until he turned to Wilder. "And what is your opinion, Mr. Wilder?"

"If you've read my file, you know my opinion," he drawled.

"Ah yes," Wainthrope declared. "Insubordinate, difficult, and argumentative."

"He's a great fighting instructor, but I prefer to listen to different opinions when it comes to politics and ethical concerns," I said, angling myself slightly in front of Wilder's increasing annoyance at the pompous Wainthrope.

The Inquisitor inclined his head. "A wise decision, Miss Ravenwood. With that attitude, perhaps we'll see you as a council member one day."

I smiled broadly, playing up to his airs and graces. Anything to get rid of him. "That would be an honour, Inquisitor. For now, I'm just excited to see the Codex."

"Of course," he replied. "I mustn't keep you from your appointment."

I nodded and stepped around him with Wilder right behind me, and we continued on our way to the conservatory.

"Miss Ravenwood?"

My heart leapt and I turned, swallowing my panic.

"I'm truly sorry for what happened to your friend,

but we must do what is necessary to maintain the balance in favour of the Light."

I wasn't naïve enough to believe he was speaking the truth, but I offered him a smile. "Of course."

His stare was long and piercing like he was peeling back the layers of my mind and fossicking around in the mess for things he could use against me. Finally, he turned and walked away.

Wilder grabbed my arm and guided me in the opposite direction towards the conservatory.

When we were out of earshot, Wilder muttered under his breath, "Self-important piece of—"

"Let it go," I interrupted. "Bigger fish to fry, remember?"

"Greer has granted you time with the Codex?" he asked, cocking his eyebrow.

"Too much?"

He grunted. "Just enough."

When we climbed the stairs into the conservatory, we found Greer and Aldrich waiting for us.

"Where's Brax?" Wilder asked as we walked in.

"We can't trust him…" Aldrich replied, "not with this."

Wilder snorted. "Finally, someone agrees with me."

"You're late," Greer stated, glancing towards the stairs. "Were you followed?"

"We ran into our favourite blonde goth rocker downstairs," I drawled.

"Wainthrope?" Aldrich asked, winning himself some serious points for understanding my reference.

I grimaced. "Don't worry, I'm pretty sure I convinced him I was a Codex junkie."

"She lied smoother than a demon on the end of a cold iron dagger," Wilder said. "Don't let her touch the Codex."

"I already have," I declared, "*twice*."

His mouth dropped open and Greer rolled her eyes. "This isn't about the code of conduct. We must protect all of us from Wainthrope's ambitions, not just Scarlett and Jackson."

She didn't have to tell me twice.

"Wainthrope will experiment on you," Aldrich said, confirming what I already feared. "He'll do whatever it takes to find Arondight and if he has to, he'll kill you in the process."

"What about Jackson?" I demanded. "What will he do to him?"

"He'll be executed tomorrow evening." Greer didn't even try to sugar-coat it.

"*No.*" My knees crumpled under the weight of our predicament and Wilder caught me before I fell. "He didn't even have a chance to defend himself!"

Greer took on a sombre expression. I was preaching to the choir.

"Ramona is certain his ability to link to the demons is malformed," she said.

"Malformed?" Wilder asked.

"When she stopped the mutation, she stopped a lot more," Greer explained, her gaze flickering to Wilder's grasp on me. "She believes the ability isn't working as it should and can be harnessed to his advantage."

"It could be to *our* advantage," I said. "We could find the Balan demon, but Wainthrope wants to kill him before Jackson can try. He just sees a threat. We need to get him out of here. Now."

"Hold on there, Purples. You're running your mouth off again. If we break him out, we'll be renegades. The whole Sanctum will declare war on our own kind...*for a demon*."

"He's right, Scarlett," Aldrich said. "We can't afford to lose Jackson, but we also can't start a civil war."

"The balance is at a critical point," Greer said. "The Codex's voice has been urgent, but so far away—"

"What did Wainthrope mean about Jackson's soul?" I asked. "Is he...damned?" I didn't even know if it was a thing, and I felt idiotic for even asking. Could someone be damned to Hell?

"He's not damned, Scarlett," Greer said. "There's no such thing as Heaven and Hell. Where the demons came from is another plane of existence."

"A parallel universe," Aldrich confirmed. "Not Hell, but I suppose that's semantics."

"Screw his soul," Wilder growled. "If he's willing to try, then we can't lose this chance to find out where that Balan is hiding."

"We agree with you, Wilder," Aldrich said. "That's why you will take Jackson and Scarlett away from the Sanctum...tonight."

Wilder glowered, but he knew as well as any of us that this had to happen now or not at all.

"We can't move openly against the Inquisitor," Greer said, placing her hand lithely on his arm. "You're the only one we trust. Without you, we could lose our only chance at stopping the balance from tipping into Darkness."

I snorted, glancing away as she used her womanly charms on the man who was head over heels for her. And they wanted to talk about the Inquisitor's manipulation? *Please.*

"Wilder doesn't have to come," I declared sullenly. "I can look out for Jackson myself. Just get us out without anyone knowing and we'll be fine."

"That's out of the question." Wilder shot me a warning glare. "Winning one fight doesn't mean you can win against Wainthrope. He has the power of the Naturals behind him. You wouldn't last an hour."

"He's right, Scarlett," Greer said.

"But you're not coming, either," I complained.

"We can do more good here than out there," Aldrich explained. "We can play Wainthrope and throw him off your scent. Buy you time to find the Balan."

It was already decided. I was standing here, but I'd never been part of the conversation.

"I'm not special," I murmured. "I've never been special."

"You've always been precious, Scarlett," Aldrich said kindly. "You just never had the chance to understand it."

"Take care of her, Wilder," Greer said. "And teach her what you can about her Light."

"Greer…" He sounded sad, like he'd been stolen away from his only chance at happiness. How deep did his feelings for her run?

I bristled at Wilder's tone and glanced away.

"The vaults are guarded by Wainthrope's men," she said brushing him off. "You'll have to get past them."

"The alarms?" he asked, narrowing his eyes.

"I'll disable them at midnight," Aldrich said. "I'll only have one chance, so make sure you're there on time."

Wilder nodded and checked his watch. "Three hours."

"Good luck." Greer placed her hands on his arm in a polite farewell. When she turned to me, I didn't know what to say. "Look to the Light," she said for me. "Trust one another, okay?"

I nodded and turned to the Codex as she left. Aldrich stood beside me, his gaze focused on the book.

"You've surprised us all, Scarlett," he said quietly. "You're quick to learn, adapt, and survive. You'll weather this, too."

He'd always had this fatherly aura around him, his wisdom and skill apparent in everything he did. Remembering the night of the breach, I shivered. I still didn't know what a Colossus was exactly, despite reading about them, but I knew he was powerful enough to take down one on his own. If Aldrich spoke, I would do well to listen.

"How do you know?"

He gave me a secretive smile and patted me on my shoulder. "I know. You remind me of someone with the same uncanny abilities." He glanced at Wilder. "Remember, midnight."

"I won't forget," he said with a curt nod.

Aldrich left us alone with the Codex and I tingled as its call reached out to the parts of me that were infused with Arondight's power.

"Did you really touch it?" Wilder asked.

"Are you concerned about me now?"

"I rebel against a lot of things, Purples. I don't exactly want to *be* a rebel, but I'm not about to let anything happen to you."

I laughed and shook my head. "The Codex calls to Arondight."

"Thought so."

"You're such a smart-arse," I grumbled. "Why can't you just say what you mean?"

"That would make it too easy for you. Besides, I was trying to figure out if this pile of steaming shite was something I wanted to get into. I got the feeling it was one of those pivotal life moments you can't go back on."

"Typical." I sighed. I then checked my arondight blade and the cold iron dagger in my boot—locked and loaded.

"Okay, Purples," Wilder drawled, checking his

weapons and flipping up the collar of his jacket, "are
you ready to stick it to The Man?"

## 10

At eleven-thirty, Wilder and I left the conservatory. We strode through the Sanctum like we owned everyone, two bad arses on the way to screw the system. Well, if anyone was actually around, we would've looked tough, but the more invisible we were, the better off we'd be.

"Remember the plan, Purples," Wilder said as we descended the stairs. "Stick to it and we'll be out of here with plenty of time to spare."

"Sure, but when did sticking to the plan ever work for us?"

"There's a first time for everything," he replied tersely.

The moment our boots hit the bottom landing, a silky voice echoed down the hall, causing my blood to freeze in my veins.

"Right. On. *Time*."

*Wainthrope*.

The Inquisitor stood in the alcove with his hands behind his back, flanked by two mean-looking Naturals from his personal squad. His smile was triumphant, as if he knew we'd try something. Were we that transparent, or did someone betray us? It didn't matter right now, but if someone had ratted on us, they'd be getting a visit from me—*if* we got out of here.

Wainthrope turned his gaze on me. "I suspected you had a flair for insubordination, Miss Ravenwood, but you're making this too easy."

"Easy?" I scoffed. "I'm a hard mountain to climb, Wainthrope."

"Conspiring to free your demon friend… That's a serious charge," he went on. "And you, Mr. Wilder. How does it feel to live up to everyone's expectations?"

"I should be asking you the same question," he replied. "Everyone thinks you're a self-serving *dick*."

"The Regula should have expelled you the day they found you on their doorstep," he stated. "Greer should never have taken you in, but it wasn't about your *ability* was it? At least not on the battlefield."

"Greer is innocent," Wilder snapped.

"Oh, of course she is," Wainthrope replied. "She'd never be allowed to touch the Codex if she wasn't. You tried to corrupt her with your pitiful attempt at loving her, but no more." He turned his cold glare onto me. "And you can't hide the truth any longer, Miss Ravenwood."

"What truth?" I asked sweetly. "That I know you're not a natural blonde?"

"And you're not a natural…*indigo*." His lips curved into a sly smile and I knew I'd been busted. "Take them into custody."

The Naturals flanking him reached for their arondight blades and I tensed.

"Well, this could've gone smoother," I drawled.

"You're preaching to the choir, Purples," Wilder replied.

"What do we do? I'm not in the mood to be a live autopsy."

"Well, we're not going to grovel, either. I'd rather asphyxiate on my own vomit."

"*Gross.*"

"Arrest them," the Inquisitor ordered, "*at once.*"

The time for hesitation was over. If the Naturals wanted me to take action, then it was time to go down in a blaze of glory.

"You know what?" I declared as the Naturals advanced. "I can't take a man with hair more luscious than mine seriously."

I reached for my Light, threw my arms up, and pushed my indigo-ness at the Inquisitor and his groupies. The air shimmered violet as a shockwave barrelled towards them, and for a split-second, Wainthrope's expression was awed. But only for a second. When the wave hit them, they flew backwards down the hall, their arms and legs flopping uselessly. Under different circumstances, it'd be hilarious, but considering I'd just attacked the leader of our people…

"Purples," Wilder said with a groan, "we have to have a serious talk about your reckless need for self-destruction."

"You can bring me down a peg or two later," I said as the Naturals hit the wall with a crash. "Now we have to break out Jackson."

I spun on my heel and ran in the opposite direction with Wilder right behind me. As we rounded the corner, the Naturals that'd been guarding Jackson's cell emerged from the vaults, searching for the source of the ruckus.

I skidded, almost causing Wilder to slam into me. They were big, beefy dudes with matching black tactical uniforms and silver arondight hilts strapped to their waists. They must have thought Jackson was a real threat if they had that kind of muscle on the door.

When they saw us, the larger guy held up his hand. "*Stop right there*. What's going on here?"

"Get out of our way and I won't hurt you," I declared, not knowing how I was going to take down two Naturals twice my size. My Light felt fuzzy after blowing away the Inquisitor and his arse-kissing friends, so I wasn't sure a repeat performance was in the cards.

They began to laugh and not even Wilder's presence seemed to sway them.

"Did you hear that?" the other guy asked his partner. "She thinks she can take us."

"Delusional," the first Natural replied.

"Better stand aside, Purples," Wilder said. "I'll deal with the ignoramuses, you get your man-toy."

The larger of the two men glowered. "Who are you calling stupid, demon spawn?"

Wilder rolled his eyes and punched the smaller guy in the face and leapt towards the other. That's when my heart jumped into my throat and I barrelled into the vaults.

The moment I pushed into the last holding cell, Jackson sat up, startled by my sudden appearance.

"Scarlett? What's going on?"

"We're breaking you out." I looked at the bars, realising there was no door. "Shit, how does this thing open?"

"We? Who's we?" He was careful not to touch the bars. Last time he was in here, the demon countermeasures had zapped him pretty hard.

"Wilder," I said, just as a loud crash echoed from outside.

"Wilder?" He looked less than impressed. "Is he blowing up the entire Sanctum out there?"

"We ran into a little…problem." I gestured wildly, then curled my hands around the bars. I shook, but they didn't budge. "How does this stupid thing open?"

Jackson leapt to his feet and pointed to the wall. "When they put me in here, they did something there. A concealed control or something."

I pressed my palms against the cool metal, but there were no breaks or hidden panels anywhere. Glancing over my shoulder, I knew I had to hurry.

Wilder couldn't hold off the guards for much longer, and Wainthrope and his posse would have recovered by now. If we didn't hustle, we'd be screwed.

"Where's a quest marker when you need one?" I asked with a groan.

"I don't know anything about this stuff, Scarlett. I—"

"*Light.*" It had to be. "Maybe if I…" I pressed my palm against the wall and reached for the purple spark inside myself. Allowing it to trickle forth, I coaxed it into the wall, searching and willing the bars to open.

Open. Open. *Open…*

A click echoed through the room and the bars began to slide up into the roof.

"Yes!" I fist-pumped the air.

Jackson rushed forwards, ducking under the retracting bars, and threw his arms around me.

"Thank you," he said. "I was afraid I was going to die in there."

"Err…" Maybe now wasn't the time to tell him he was right. "We can hug it out later. Right now, we need to leg it."

Out in the hall, Wilder was still fighting the two Natural guards, but something wasn't right. He dodged their blows with ease, but he wasn't striking back. He was…*toying* with them like a cat played with a mouse.

"Stop playing with your food!" I exclaimed.

He smirked, then dropped the first guy with a well-aimed punch, then he spun, blasting the second with his Light. The Natural flew down the hall, colliding with Wainthrope and his guards, toppling them a second time.

"What a show off," Jackson declared.

"Follow me," Wilder said, ignoring Jackson. "Keep him between us."

"How are we getting out?" I asked as we sprinted away from the tangled pile of Naturals.

"Service entrance," Wilder threw over his shoulder. "We've got five minutes before the alarms are rearmed."

"Traitors!" Wainthrope bellowed behind us. "Don't let them escape!"

"Oh shite!" Jackson exclaimed. "Oh shite! Shite, shite, *shite*—"

"Will you shut the hell up and run?" Wilder exclaimed.

I shoved Jackson in front of me and we bolted, knowing that behind us, the Inquisitor was untangling himself from another pile of Naturals.

When we reached the stairwell at the very back of the building, I was surprised when Wilder led us down instead of up. I'd never gone down before, and honestly, I never knew there was more below the vaults.

We thundered down the stairs and pushed into the basement. A huge boiler sat at one side, and a mass of electrical cables snaked across the ceiling, following a trail of shiny silver ductwork. There were panels and machines, and high-voltage signs everywhere. We were firmly in the belly of the beast, so to speak.

"There's no way out of here," I said. "We're underground."

Wilder didn't reply. He just led us across the basement and through a door hidden at the rear. Inside, I felt a cool breeze tickle my flushed skin. Breathing in, I almost threw up as the rancid scent of something dead or dying flew into my nostrils.

"Oh gods," I exclaimed. "What's that?"

"Shite," Wilder said with a shrug.

"Did he just say shite?" Jackson asked, following us into the room. He immediately gagged.

In the centre of the dank little room sat an iron manhole cover with the words 'sewer' stamped into the iron. It wasn't completely solid, so the stench had plenty of air holes from which to escape and attack our noses. No wonder it'd been locked away in this little corner.

"The sewer?" I asked, raising my eyebrows. "Really?"

"We can't just walk out the front door," Wilder replied. "Besides, this exit isn't well known. Aldrich told me about it. The Sanctum was built over the old city and even older buildings. Misalignments were bound to happen."

"I can see why no one comes down here," Jackson said. "It reeks."

"Service entrance usually means a loading dock, not a toilet cistern," I added. "Seriously, do the alarms and glamours reach all the way down here?"

"Yes."

I glanced over my shoulder as Wilder pried open

the heavy iron grate in the floor. The metal scraped back, making an awful racket, and he gestured for us to drop down into the darkness.

"The point of no return passed a long time ago," Wilder said. "Let's go."

Holding my breath, I climbed into the gaping maw of darkness, my feet fumbling for the ladder rungs I knew protruded from the stone. It wasn't that deep, so when I reached the bottom, I stepped back and waited for the others.

The tunnel was reinforced with massive stone slabs, marking it somewhere around the Victorian era. Unfortunately, the stink wasn't that of fossilised human waste, but something a lot juicer. This particular tunnel was still in use, maybe from the Sanctum or surrounding industrial buildings. Just our luck.

Jackson landed next to me, followed by Wilder, who dragged the grate back into place before jumping off the ladder.

He hit the cobblestones with a squelch, causing us to gag.

"I think I just stood on a turd," Jackson moaned.

"We don't need the commentary," Wilder hissed, moving off into the darkness. How he knew which way to go was anyone's guess.

"Quiet," I urged my best friend. "Who knows how sound travels down here."

Jackson took on a sheepish look and followed close behind me. He might be an enhanced human with muscles, super hearing, and all the things, but he was still that nerdy gamer guy I'd met all those years ago.

Wilder turned on the torch on his mobile phone, lighting our way. We kept moving, the sewer angling slightly down as we went. It had to open out some place—I mean, shit had to go somewhere right?

Every so often, another passage flowed into the main channel, the openings covered in massive iron grates. Our footsteps splashed and squelched, and I was forced to cover my nose with my sleeve. Poor Jackson must be regretting his enhanced sense of smell right about now, but I supposed anything was better than a public execution.

It wasn't long before a murky shadow appeared ahead. Outside, it was still the middle of the night, so the overwhelming artificial lights of the city were bleeding into the sewer.

When we finally emerged onto the banks of the Thames, squeezing through the rusted grate that blocked the exit, I breathed in the clear air and scraped my boots against the stony shore. Thank goodness the tide was out, otherwise we'd have to swim.

"What now?" Jackson asked, staring up at the starry sky.

"We find somewhere to regroup," I replied. "Wherever that is."

"I know a place," Wilder said, tossing his phone into the water. The Naturals might be supernatural, but it didn't mean they didn't know how to wrangle technology. "But it's on the other side of the city."

"*Great*. It isn't like everyone's looking for us or anything."

"Calm your farm, Purples," he drawled. "We'll be safe there. No amount of Light will be able to find us once we're inside."

"Where is this magical place?" Jackson asked, narrowing his eyes. "Narnia?"

"No," Wilder said, walking off, "Finsbury Park."

## 11

S taring at the empty lot, I blinked.

Jackson stood next to me, looking perplexed, and Wilder just seemed proud of his accomplishments. I hoped the was one epic glamour because the grass was at least a metre high—and probably home to various critters and creepy crawlies I didn't want to believe existed.

Once we'd found our way across the Thames, we'd hitched a ride in a cab all the way to Finsbury Park. Technically it was Harringay, but the line between locals was so blurry, it didn't seem to matter. Anyway, Wilder had used alteration on the driver, otherwise he'd remember us, but I suspected it had more to do with the guy refusing the fare because we reeked of *you know what*.

"Are we camping?" Jackson drawled. "Because it looks to me that your fancy hideout doesn't exist. Unless it's an underground bunker."

"There are a lot of old World War II-era air-raid

shelters hidden around the city," Wilder said. "You'd be surprised."

"Please don't tell me this is one of them," I said. "I need a hot shower."

Wilder rolled his eyes. "Of course not. I'm not a Neanderthal."

"*Could've fooled me*," Jackson muttered under his breath, earning himself a sharp elbow in the ribs from me.

Luckily for him, Wilder didn't hear. The Natural strode forwards, climbed a set of invisible stairs, and lifted his hand. To our surprise, a door opened in front of him, revealing the interior of a house.

I drew in a sharp breath. "It's glamoured."

Gesturing for us to follow, Wilder said, "You better come in before the neighbours see."

Jackson tilted from side to side in an attempt to get his head around what he was seeing. "How do I know where the steps are?"

"Guesstimate," I replied, feeling the way with my Natural senses.

I brushed past Wilder as I entered the house, not at all surprised when I found the inside to be just as abrasive as the man himself. The wallpaper was peeling, the stairs were crooked, the floorboards were warped, and that was just the things I could see from where I stood.

"*Ow!*"

Turning, I was just in time to see Jackson scrambling to his feet. He'd tripped over the steps.

"For an enhanced human, you're pretty uncoordinated," Wilder drawled.

"Scarlett, you seriously like this guy?"

I shrugged as Wilder hauled him into the house and closed the door.

"Why wouldn't you tell anyone about this place?" I asked as we moved into the front room. "What do you need to escape from?"

"You're really asking me that question?" His eyebrows rose as he flicked on the lights. "I'm the guy who was branded as demon spawn for being different."

"I know all about that," Jackson drawled.

Wilder narrowed his eyes. "I had to have someplace secret as a contingency plan. I've been tolerated all these years, but I always believed one day that tolerance would run out."

"But you're a Natural," I argued. "There's no demon in you."

"It doesn't matter."

"I hate to say it, but he's right," Jackson declared. "People can be real mean when they want to be."

"Wonders never cease," Wilder drawled before shucking off his jacket.

Glancing around the room, I took everything in. It felt like a bunch of art students from the local college rented the place. The formal living room was sparsely furnished with a mismatch of modern flatpack pieces and antique relics. The couch looked like it was nicked out of an Elizabethan-era manor house, and the coffee table was black Ikea chipboard. The rug was one of those elaborate Turkish designs, its authenticity debatable, and it was worn down to the canvas in places.

"You don't happen to have some spare clothes lying around?" Jackson asked, staring at the peeling wallpaper. "I've been stuck in these for days."

"There's spare stuff in the next room," Wilder said. "They should fit now that you've reached puberty and filled out some."

"*Wilder*," I scolded.

"I broke his arse out of the vaults, I think I've earned a few well-timed one-liners, Purples."

"Whatever," Jackson said. "I'm just glad to get out of these clothes." Before Wilder could reply, he pushed out of the room.

Listening to his boots echo down the hall, I shook my head at Wilder with disapproval.

"What?" he asked, shrugging. "He makes it too easy."

I didn't say anything as he moved to the front window. I was too tired to argue and too worried about someone finding us before I had the chance to shower, let alone get my head around our next move.

"Did you cloak the house?" I asked, watching as Wilder peered through the curtains.

"Yeah. I've built it up over the years, so the cloak is so thick, nothing can see through it."

"Not even other Naturals?"

"There's a slim chance, but they'd have to know what they're looking for."

It wasn't entirely reassuring, but he seemed confident. It wasn't like we had other options.

I stood next to him and checked out the street. Nothing moved on the orange-tinted road, and all the houses in the row were dark and silent. A mist had crept in at some point, though the sky was clear.

"Ugh. How did we get here?" I mused, rubbing my tired eyes.

"We walked."

"Ha ha, very funny."

Wilder smirked. "It's my fall-back career."

Pressing my flushed forehead against the cool window pane, I began to dwell on how rapidly things had changed. One day I was a nobody working behind the bar at a pub, the next my best friend had been mutated by a demon and we were on the run. It was fair to say I'd never aspired to perform a jail break.

"It's ironic, don't you think?" I mused out loud.

"What is?"

"I wanted to be a part of something," I replied, my fingers brushing against my arondight blade. "But I ended up being a renegade and a fugitive. *The irony.*"

"Now don't go getting a big head, Purples."

"Why are you always so mean to me?" I asked, glaring at him. "Am I that much of a pain in your arse?"

"No," he replied, "you're not."

"Then why?"

"I suppose it's something that's developed from all

those years of people treating me like I was a disease. After a while, you expect it from everyone."

"Not everyone is like that."

"I know."

"I'm not like that." I eyed him, a flare of jealousy taking over my mouth. "Greer isn't like that."

His gaze darkened. "Greer has to be impartial because of her position."

"Does she feel the same?"

"*Scarlett.*" His tone was dangerous, and I bristled.

"What? Even Wainthrope knew."

"It doesn't mean it's open for discussion."

I sighed and clamped my mouth shut. Maybe Greer couldn't feel the same because of who she was. As the protector of the Codex, it must be frowned upon if she was fraternising with a rebellious anomaly. It was exactly who I was, so what did that make the two of us together?

"*Sorry,*" I drawled, turning my gaze out over the city. "Forget about it. Just go back to calling me Purples and being a dick."

"You challenge authority at every step, have a smart-arse comeback for everything, have an unnatural ability to excel where you should flounder, and you've inspired danger and insubordination from the moment I met you."

I made a face. "Sounds like I should get an A-plus with honours."

"I'm trying to make you a better warrior, Scarlett. It's not just about fighting with your body, it's your mind I'm trying to hone. This world isn't easy on a good day, and it's even worse for people like us. The head *must* rule over the heart."

"The different amongst the different."

He nodded. "We'll always be fighting something. If it isn't demons, it's prejudice, jealousy…" he plucked at a strand of my violet hair, "those hungry for power." *Like Julius Wainthrope.* "The days of reckless risk taking are over, *Purples.* This war—"

"You don't have to say it," I said, turning so he was forced to drop the strand of hair he was stroking. "We've taken the first steps into the End Times." Capitalised, because it was the dawning of a new age.

Wilder grunted and turned his glare onto the street below. I followed his gaze, my Light fizzing around the edges. We'd never had much of a chance to practice at the Sanctum, let alone talk about what'd happened at our first training session. Now wasn't the greatest time to bring it up, but there never was a dull moment of late.

"We never talked about our Light," I said. "How it seemed to melt together." I'd used it recklessly tonight *again*, and I still felt like I was lacking in the control department. Reality was, I kept dabbling in things I didn't understand, and I couldn't afford to get soul sick now that we were on our own. "From the look on your face, I'm pretty sure that never happens."

"It was an anomaly," Wilder stated. "Your Light is unpredictable because of—"

"Arondight," I said, my irritableness getting the better of me. "Yeah, yeah, I know."

"You're also untrained, though you seem to have an irritating knack for blowing things away."

I snorted, covering my mouth.

"You shouldn't laugh, Purples."

"You have to admit seeing Wainthrope fly down that hallway was funny as hell."

His lips quirked, just a little, but he didn't allow his amusement to show any further. Sometimes I wished he'd just let go of all the surly, but I knew it was just a deep-rooted self-preservation thing. One day, I'd get him to come out of his murky solitude.

"Here." He took my hand and wove his fingers through mine.

My breath caught at the unexpected touch and I cursed silently. I couldn't have feelings for Wilder. I mean, he had a hard-on for Greer and that made his attentions so completely unobtainable it wasn't even funny. I was the irritating thorn in his side, and now I was the reason he was on the run from his—*our*—own people.

"Try calling for your Light again," he murmured.

I closed my eyes, hiding my flushed cheeks behind a curtain of purple hair. Reaching inside myself, I felt the spark of my power and called it forth. Just a little. It was much easier now that I knew what to look for. Instinct was one thing, but using Light with deliberate intent was a tough skill to master.

I felt Wilder's silver Light flare and reached out tentatively.

"Good," he said. "This is better."

"I think I get it now," I replied.

The edges of my Light brushed against Wilder's and tendrils snaked out and began to entwine. It wasn't just me, but him as well.

"Scarlett," he warned.

"I'm not doing it by myself," I hissed.

"*Ahem.*"

I pulled my hand from Wilder's at the sound of Jackson's irritated cough. He stood just inside the room, smirking at us and I had to do a double-take. Tight black T-shirt, check. Black jeans with ripped knees, check. Combat boots, check. If it wasn't for his pasty skin and wild mop of curly hair, I would've been looking at a creepy Wilder clone.

"Do you really like wearing tight T-shirts?" he asked Wilder, pulling at the fabric. "Because it's cutting off my circulation."

Ignoring Jackson, Wilder looked at me. "You want to go next?"

"You go," I replied. "I don't trust you two together. I'm likely to come back and find you at each other's throats."

He grunted and strode from the room, knocking his shoulder against Jackson's as he went.

I sighed, crossing my arms over my chest.

Jackson glowered. "Irritated I caught you playing handsies with Mr. Grumpy?"

I shook my head. "It wasn't like that."

"Then what was it like? Enlighten me." Making sure the door was closed, he moved towards me.

"I'm trying to figure out my Light," I fired back. "Every time I get a chance to try to control it, something or someone interrupts. At this point, it's getting real frustrating."

"Sounds like the sexual tension in this place," he drawled.

"*Jackson.*"

"Thanks for busting me out of death row, by the way."

My shoulders slumped. "You got that, hey?"

"That Inquisitor guy came to see me," he went on. "He's got a real issue with demons. I mean, I can't blame him, but it's not like I ever wanted to be one."

"I know. Greer and Aldrich know, too."

"And Wilder?" He raised his eyebrows.

"Him, too."

"He doesn't like me," he stated. "He's very patronising, you know."

I shrugged. "That's Wilder in a nutshell."

"You'd think we'd have something in common with the whole demon thing."

"I wouldn't bring it up," I warned. "You're likely to get your head knocked off."

"By his fist or his irresistible charm?"

I snorted and sank down onto the couch, my muscles screaming. "Oi, I'm wrecked."

Jackson sat beside me, smelling like spicy soap and a little Wilder-esque. "You're not worried I'm still linked to that demon guy, are you?"

I shook my head. "I trust Ramona. She said the ability was malformed."

He scrunched his nose. "Malformed?"

"It didn't develop right," I explained, pushing him

lightly on the arm. I was still impressed at the size of his muscles considering he didn't do any work to get them. "The only reason you were able to see him was because she stimulated the…well, whatever it is inside you."

"Barry," he declared.

"Huh?"

"I like to call my demon growth Barry."

I laughed and turned to face him, glad we were back to that easy place our relationship had always been in. "You're so weird."

He smiled, his lips pulling up to one side.

"You've changed," I murmured.

"Is that a good thing? All things considered, I mean."

"You seem more sure of yourself, *all things considered*."

"Scarlett…" his gaze lowered, "do you ever wonder…"

"Wonder what?"

He leaned forward and pressed his lips against mine, capturing me in a soft kiss. Startled, and a little caught in the moment, I fisted my hand into his T-shirt and kissed him back. His tongue caught mine and for a blistering second, I almost wished I could pretend. But then I tensed, disappointed. It was a nice kiss, I couldn't fault him on technique, but…

Jackson pulled back, sensing the change in my touch, his breath heavy. "That wasn't right, was it?" he asked with a frown.

I shook my head apologetically. "Nope."

The door opened and Wilder strolled in, his hair damp. Looking at us, he cocked an eyebrow.

"What?" I made a face.

"Shower's free, Purples," he said. "There's a bed next door and one upstairs. You two choose which one you want."

"What about you?" I asked, shucking off my jacket.

"I'll be fine here." He returned to the window, but not before flashing a strange look at Jackson.

"What's our next move?" Jackson asked, rising to his feet. For the first time, I realised the two men stood at the same height and their builds were similar thanks to Jackson's enhancement. "I mean, we can't play house for long. That demon's not going to wait around."

"That's something to worry about tomorrow," Wilder said. "For now, get some rest."

Jackson nodded and placed his hand on my shoulder. "I'll take upstairs, okay?"

"Yeah."

I lingered as Jackson's footsteps echoed up the rickety stairs to the second floor. Wilder turned, tilting his head to the side.

"Wilder—"

"You better get cleaned up, Purples," he declared. "Better make it quick, though. I can't promise there'll be much hot water left."

Thankfully for him, he wasn't in hitting distance. "*Great.* Thanks a lot."

12

*Scarlett, you have to hide, okay?*

Invisible hands smoothed down my hair. *You're so brave, sweetie.*

I jerked awake, sitting up in the unfamiliar bed with a start. My heart beat a wild rhythm in my chest and I clutched Wilder's T-shirt against my skin. It was the same dream again. The one with my parents and the Balan demon.

The dream where they died.

My gaze focused on the plastered wall and the closet with the broken door. *I was at Wilder's redneck row house.*

Swinging my legs out of bed, I rose and did some stretches, wondering if the others were up.

Checking out the closet now that it was light out, I didn't find anything interesting. The only thing inside was Wilder's standard uniform of black trousers and matching T-shirts. None of the bottoms fit me, so I grabbed a clean T-shirt for later. I also didn't have any makeup, but I'd stopped wearing it weeks ago, and how my skin thanked me. My freckled English pallor really shone through lately.

The sun was well and truly up when I finally shuffled into the kitchen at the back of the house. My bare feet were cold against the rough floorboards, but it was doing wonders in helping me wake up.

Wilder was leaning against the counter, eating baked beans straight from the can. When I walked in, he raised an eyebrow. "Did you forget your trousers?"

"No." I pouted and sat down at the table. "You know, baked beans make you fart."

He snorted and nodded towards the cupboards. "There's more in there if you want some. We can start an orchestra."

The sound of Jackson's footsteps on the stairs drove us to silence. Wilder glanced at my bare legs, then grunted.

"What?" I demanded.

Jackson appeared in the kitchen, sniffing the air, and interrupting whatever was on Wilder's mind. "I can smell beans."

Wilder nodded to the cupboards. "Knock yourself out."

Jackson began to open all the doors and check out the contents with no shame.

"This place is like a nuclear fallout shelter," he said. "Canned food, powdered mash, powdered milk, bottled water…" He pulled out a can and held it up. "*Oohh*, spaghetti in the shape of dinosaurs."

I threw a look at Wilder who just smirked. "Tesco had them on special."

"You're seriously weird," I drawled. I couldn't picture Wilder wheeling a shopping trolley up and down the aisles of a supermarket, let alone how he got it all back here.

"People always forget about the food when they go underground. We leave, we become detectable. No way I'm risking running into Wainthrope because I really wanted a kebab. Besides," he grinned lopsidedly at me, "I knew this place would come in handy one day."

"Well, aren't you clever."

Jackson was busy opening the can of dinosaur spaghetti. "Wake up on the wrong side of the bed this morning?"

"I couldn't sleep," I replied, rubbing my eyes. "Old memories."

"You're dreaming again?"

"What dream?" Wilder asked, straightening up.

"Nothing," I muttered. "It's nothing."

"Of course it's something."

"You didn't care about the last one." I glanced at Jackson, who was devouring cold dinosaur spaghetti by the spoonful. *Gross*.

Wilder grunted. "I didn't want to worry you, there's a difference."

"It's about her parents," my best friend said, his mouth still full.

"Thanks a lot," I said, finishing off with a curse.

Wilder's eyes narrowed slightly, but he didn't press

any further. "You should eat something. It'll make you feel better. There are plenty of dinosaurs for everyone."

I shook my head and focused on the back garden. The grass was overgrown, and a few nettle bushes rustled against the glass.

Joking about the food situation was all well and good, but we were on the run from our own people, had a whole host of demons on our arses, and none of us seemed to have any idea where to go next. How did people find greater demons? Somehow, I didn't think there was such a thing as a locator spell. Naturals weren't witches…were we?

"We need to talk about our next step," Wilder said. "We can't wait."

"That guy you're looking for was seriously creepy," Jackson stated. "He was covered in blood and sewing bits of flesh together with one of those little needles. It was like Frankenstein's monster on acid."

"That's how Balan demons roll."

I shuddered, my vision filling with imagined images of a red room and a monster stitched together with intestines sticking out of crudely sewn flesh.

"How are we going to find him when the entire London Sanctum couldn't turn up the slightest whiff?" I asked with a shudder. I couldn't see a way, other than offering myself up as bait and luring him out into the open. Somehow, I knew Wilder wouldn't go for it. They'd tried that before and the results had been disastrous.

"I can try to use Barry," Jackson offered.

Wilder scowled. "Who the hell is Barry?"

"My demon growth," he replied with a shrug.

"You named your mutation?"

"He's weird like that," I said.

"You think you can access it?" Wilder asked, pulling out a chair and sitting beside me. "Without the help of electric shock?"

It was Jackson's turn to shrug. "I have no idea how to control it, or if it works both ways, but it's worth a try."

"No," I said. "Last time you convulsed for a full minute. I don't want you to go through that again."

"That's because Ramona activated an ability with an electrical current that was too powerful for it," Wilder stated. "If he can activate it with his mind, it should work."

"How do I do that?"

Wilder shrugged. "Probably the same way we use our Light."

"It's too risky," I argued.

"I'm going to have to disagree with you, Scarlett," my best friend declared. "Considering what's at stake here, and our leads are at zero, it's worth it."

"You won't be safe until we can kill that Balan," Wilder added.

"I'll never be safe," I snapped. "There'll always be someone who wants to take advantage of me because of Arondight."

"Probably," Wilder said with a shrug. "But one less greater demon in the world doesn't hurt, either."

I wasn't getting any sympathy from Wilder, that

was for sure. Turning to Jackson, I scowled. "You can't be serious about this."

"You know we're right. As much as I like dinosaur spaghetti, we can't stay here forever."

Wilder nodded his agreement. "This place won't remain hidden for long, Purples. I'm good, but nothing is one hundred percent impenetrable."

"So we have to go out there and track the demon," Jackson said, "before he can track us."

"You catch on quick," Wilder drawled. "There's hope for you yet."

"I'll take that as a compliment."

"Of course it was a compliment, just don't get used to it." Wilder turned his silver eyes on me. "Things have amped up out there and it's only been twelve hours since we left the Sanctum."

"How do you know?" I asked.

"The cloak on the house dampens it, but you can feel the Darkness in the air," he replied. "Everything's hazy and you can feel a weight pressing down on your back. They know what we did last night, and they're searching for us…especially you, Purples."

"Me? What about you?"

"We're expendable," Jackson replied for him. "It's Arondight they really want."

"Wainthrope knows who you are now," Wilder added. "He'll do anything to get his hands on you." *And pry me open with Light to find the whereabouts of their stupid purple sword.*

"It doesn't mean you have to risk your lives on your own," I argued.

"*Scarlett,*" Wilder said, placing his hands on my face.

It was an intimate touch, and I froze, my heart leaping. When did our relationship change? It hadn't, not really. He was just using what he already suspected to get me to stop arguing with him. *Low blow.*

"Whatever you do, don't leave the house," he said.

"I'm pretty sure there's mould in the walls," I argued, twisting out of his grasp. "What if a spore gets stuck in my lungs?"

"When was the last time you were sick, Purples? Ever catch a cold?"

I screwed up my face, trying to recall last winter, and the one before that.

"She's never been sick in the whole time I've known her," Jackson said before he turned to me to cut my argument from my lips. "And hangovers don't count, Scarlett."

"We've got great immune systems," Wilder declared. "If something kills you, it won't be black mould."

"*That's so reassuring.*"

"We'll be fine, Scarlett," Jackson said. "Wilder's a wizard, and I'm genetically enhanced."

"A crack demon hunting team," Wilder drawled.

"Are you sure you aren't going to kill one another?" I asked with a groan. "I'm worried about the demons *and* Wainthrope, but you two together… Are you sure you don't need a mediator?"

"You're staying here, Purples."

"But—"

"Do I have to give you homework?"

Jackson sniggered, earning himself one of my best dirty looks.

I shook my head. "How will I know you're all right?"

Wilder smiled and gave my bare knee a reassuring squeeze. "If we're not back by midnight, *the spaghetti's all yours.*"

***

The house was deathly quiet without Jackson and Wilder in it.

I lowered into a squat and watched my clothes spin in the washing machine. The barrel whirred as it turned, hypnotising and drawing me into its depths.

After a can of dinosaur spaghetti and an afternoon of laundry, there was still no word from the two men. I hated not knowing what was going on, if they were in trouble, or if they'd found something, or if they'd been captured—by demons *or* the Inquisitor's cronies.

Once my trousers were dry, I got dressed and went snooping. I found a woollen jumper in the front room and shucked it over my T-shirt, inhaling eau de Wilder. There were holes in the stitching, but it was warm. The heating was out, and when I went into the basement to check out the boiler, I'd found lots of evidence that spiders were waiting to ambush, so I'd legged it back upstairs, not keen on being eaten by a Daddy Longlegs.

I lingered by the front window and peered out at the street beyond. A car trundled past, then a guy on a bike, then a woman walking a dog. But nothing else stirred.

The sun set at four p.m. If it wasn't for the orange hue of the street lamps, the darkness would've been absolute. The longer I watched the city, and used my spirit, the more I understood what Wilder had said earlier. The demons were out and about, their Darkness pushing at the balance with the brute force of a battering ram.

When a little car drove past with a Christmas tree strapped to the roof, I had to stop myself. Was it December already? I cuddled into Wilder's jumper and sighed. I felt more detached from my old life and the regular human world with each day that passed.

The holidays seemed frivolous compared to the odds we were currently facing. Carols, gingerbread, roast dinners, presents… Thinking about the dinosaur spaghetti, I snorted. What I wouldn't give for a little plum pudding right about now.

Sighing, I let the curtains fall back into place.

A crash tore through the perfect stillness and my heart leapt into my throat. Cold air blasted through the house as Wilder and Jackson barrelled into the front room.

Jackson's arm was flung over Wilder's neck and his legs dragged as the Natural practically carried him inside. The front of my best friend's T-shirt was dark with blood, and his skin was tinted an odd shade of grey.

I stepped forwards, my heart twisting, and I knew I should've gone with them.

Something had gone terribly wrong. *Big time.*

**13**

—————

Wilder flung Jackson down onto the couch and fell to his knees beside him.

"What the hall happened out there?" I demanded, my anxiety through the roof.

He ignored me, shoving my best friend's T-shirt up. A nasty gash tore across Jackson's stomach, blood seeping out of the torn flesh in time with his accelerated heartbeat. I didn't have to be a genius to know that gut wounds equalled a slow death.

I fell to my knees beside them and reached out.

"Don't touch him," Wilder snapped.

"Why?" I asked, yanking back my hand. "What's wrong?"

"It's Barry," Jackson rasped.

I frowned. "Barry?"

Wiping his forehead with the back of his arm, Wilder said, "I tried to patch him, but his mutation won't allow my Light to mesh."

Jackson grimaced as his stomach muscles tensed. "It also looks like my blood is acidic to human flesh."

"It's got to be an immune response to the trauma," Wilder said. "Otherwise Ramona would have mentioned it."

"What can we do?" We didn't break him out of the Sanctum only for this to happen barely a day later. After everything Jackson had been through, for his life to end like this…? It was cruel.

Wilder lowered his gaze, the surly smart-arse nowhere to be seen. "I don't know."

"Not like this," I said as tears filled my eyes. "I wasn't even there!"

"It's okay, Scarlett," Jackson rasped. "We tried."

I looked at the wound, then at him, and shook my head. I'd always been a little stubborn, I guess that's why I made such an amazing foster kid growing up. *Not.*

I scowled and flexed my fingers. "*Not hard enough.*"

"Scarlett!" Wilder shouted, but it was too late.

I pressed both palms across the tear in Jackson's gut and pushed my Light into his body. My hands began to sizzle as his blood went on the attack and I grimaced, the scent of burning flesh filling my nostrils. Hissing, I ignored the pain and used instinct to guide me.

"Why didn't you let me go!" I cried, blood seeping through my fingers. Was it my imagination or was steam rising from my boiling flesh?

My vision began to blur and I hunched forwards. I had no idea what I was doing. Reckless, insubordinate…I was living up to Wainthrope's assessment all right. I wasn't special. They had it all wrong.

Just as I was about to pass out, Wilder's hand pressed on my shoulder and I felt his power flare before it entwined with my indigo strands.

I gasped, my eyes flying open as a twist of purple and silver electricity sparked down my arms and shot into Jackson. His body jerked as he let out a strangled cry.

Panicking, I almost severed the connection, but I couldn't let go, not now. Something was happening. Jackson's blood stopped eating away at my skin, and I sensed his mutation retreat.

"It's working," I muttered, my strength fading. "*It's working.*"

"That's enough," Wilder said. "He's healing on his own now."

I shook my head.

"*Scarlett.*" He took his hand off my shoulder, severing the connection between our Light.

I fell backwards, hitting the floor with an *oomph*. I cradled my seared palms against my chest and whimpered.

"Jackson?"

"He's out," Wilder said, kneeling over me.

"I hope that's good because I have no idea what we just did."

He grasped my wrists and inspected the burns, his expression unreadable. It didn't matter what he thought, though, I knew it was bad. My flesh burned like I'd touched the sun with my bare skin. Like Icarus, I'd gotten too close.

"That was stupid as hell," Wilder growled.

"So was adding your Light to mine." Especially when we still didn't know why it reacted the way it did. I'm sure he'd explain it away because of *Arondight*.

He grabbed at my wrists, pulling my hands to where he could see them.

"The hell…" His eyes widened.

"What? Can you see bone?" My stomach rolled, the pain throbbing even more at the thought of infection and skeletal fingers. "I feel sick."

"Purples, you keep surprising me." He ran his fingers over my palms, sending a different kind of shiver up and down my spine. One I wasn't expecting.

I stared at my hands as my skin changed in front of my eyes. *I was healing.* "I don't understand."

"Whatever we did to Jackson must've flowed back into you."

"*Wow.*"

"Don't make it a regular thing," he drawled, his dry demeanour coming back to the surface. "We're dealing with things we don't understand but pretend that we do."

I pushed myself to my knees and looked at Jackson. His eyes were closed, and his chest rose with steady breaths.

Wilder picked up the blanket that'd fallen to the floor and draped it over him, then looked to me. "Let's get you cleaned up."

He helped me into the tiny bathroom and sat me

on the toilet while he filled the bath with steaming water.

"I can clean myself up, thank you," I grumbled.

He narrowed his eyes in warning. "Nice jumper. Where'd you find that?"

"Some arsehole left it on the floor."

His lips quirked and he dipped a face washer into the water. Wringing it out, he rubbed at the blood on my palms, closely inspecting my skin. There wasn't much room to manoeuvre, which made for extremely close quarters. I mean, it wasn't like we hadn't wrestled and beat each other up in training, but this felt different. Wilder actually seemed to care. Not about what I could do for the Naturals, but about *me*, and he wasn't even trying to cover it up with one of his trademark sarcastic jokes.

"Am I going to live?" I joked awkwardly.

"It would seem so…"

I took a deep breath, pushing my complicated feelings aside. "What happened out there?"

"I think we were on the right track and they weren't happy about it." He dipped the face washer back into the bath and wrung it out, leaving red swirls in the water.

"Jackson was able to tap into his abilities?"

Wilder nodded. "It was patchy at best, but all we had. It was like he had a sense of where demons were lingering, but it kept phasing in and out. Sometimes it was strong, other times it was weak."

"Like how I can sense you sometimes?" I mused.

"Yeah."

"What attacked you?"

"It was a lesser demon, but it was frenzied. Got the jump on us." I couldn't imagine anything getting past Wilder.

"Frenzied?" I frowned, wanting to take the face washer off him, but part of me was content to let him continue rubbing at the blood on my skin.

"They're everywhere," he murmured. "There's an excessive amount of possession and body jumping—more than I've ever seen. There was a *desperation* to it."

"They're looking for us," I murmured, tugging my hands away, "for Arondight."

"They're casting a net and before long, we'll be caught." And that wasn't even mentioning Wainthrope's Naturals.

"We need another plan…" If we didn't find a way to stop the Balan demon, they'll just keep coming. He was the one controlling all of this, I felt it in the air. The heaviness had a familiar stench to it. *Scarlett, you have to hide, okay?*

I hissed and rubbed my palms against my temples. Wilder tensed. "Scarlett?"

"The dream about my parents. There's a reason I had it again." I screwed my eyes shut, but it did nothing to clear away the sick feeling in my stomach. "I had it twice when I first met you. Then again last night."

"It could mean a lot of things."

"I don't know what to do," I cried, the dam of emotions I'd been bottling up breaking open. "I'm screwing up everything. I ruined Jackson's life, I messed up yours, I keep putting my foot in the proverbial pile of shite, and I'm supposed to be… I don't know what I'm supposed to be!"

"Purples," Wilder murmured, capturing my wrists before I smacked him in the face with all my flailing. "You're doing just fine. It's an unfamiliar world, I get it, but you can't fall apart on me now." He let my wrists go and retrieved the face washer. "Jackson mutating wasn't your fault and my life was already screwed up well before I met you. You didn't ask to be touched by Arondight, either. It all comes back to that Balan. We kill him and all our immediate problems go away, and if we're lucky, the balance just might tip a little to the Light for a change."

He started washing off the rest of the blood on my hands, then scrubbed his own. I watched him, numb with exhaustion. I'd zapped my Light again, falling just short of empty.

"How?" I whispered. "We're three people against a whole army. The Dark *and* the Light are looking for us."

"I have an idea," he replied, emptying the bath. "For now, you and Jackson need to rest. You seriously dulled your Light."

I grunted and sank my hands into the sleeves of Wilder's jumper. My palms felt tender and the skin was a little pink, but they didn't hurt anymore. It was a neat trick, but I better not rely on it if it gave me a hangover like this.

"Help me drag the mattress from the bedroom into the front," I said. "I want us to stay together."

His brow creased, but he didn't try to talk me out of it. Instead, he said, "I'll take care of it."

Even after the day and night he'd had roaming the streets of London with my demon detector best friend, he still had the strength to manoeuvre a queen-sized mattress down a narrow hall and through an English-sized door. Whoever had built this house had done so in a time when people were tinier and had terrible health care.

I propped myself against the front window, one eye on the darkened street and one on Wilder as he arranged the mattress on the floor. My feet were cold, my toes curling around the edge of the worn rug, touching the floorboards.

"Mind if I share one half?" he asked, dumping a pile of pillows and blankets on the floor.

"Whatever." I watched Jackson's chest rise and fall. He was deathly still.

Wilder followed my gaze. "He's going to be okay, Purples. He just needs to sleep it off."

"I know."

"What's got your knickers in a twist, then?"

"What if Arondight did something to me?" I asked. "Something more than just turning my Light purple."

"Even if it did, it has to be a good thing. It protected you from the Codex and saved your man-toy's life."

I snorted and climbed onto the mattress and pulled the covers up. "Any power can be used for evil."

"Then don't get carried away." Wilder kicked off his boots and fisted his hand into the back of his T-shirt, tugging it up and over his head. "People's choices make them good or evil, not contact with some sword."

I felt my cheeks flush as my gaze fell to his muscled torso. "So you think even demons could have a chance at being good?"

"This is too deep a conversation after such an intense day, Purples." He grinned down at me and I turned onto my back, my gaze finding the ceiling. "Like what you see?" he teased.

"The cut on your side is still a little pink." The gash he'd gotten fighting the Balan in the incursion was healed, but still sliced a path across his waist.

"I hear chicks dig scars." The mattress dipped beside me.

"Not when you get them from demons, they don't."

"Worried about me?"

"Don't push your luck."

"You weren't meant to do that, you know."

"Do what?"

"Heal Jackson like that."

I grunted. "We did it together."

"Maybe."

I turned over, glancing up at Jackson before I closed my eyes.

There was nothing else to say.

Wilder was already up by the time I opened my eyes.

I hadn't had any more dreams, which was a welcomed relief. Jerking awake and calling out for my mummy wasn't exactly something I wanted my tough warrior mentor to see. I'd had enough emotional moments in front of him as it was.

"Hey," Jackson murmured.

Rolling over, I smiled. "Hey, yourself."

"Sleep okay?"

"Yeah. I needed it." My gaze flickered to his stomach.

"I'm okay," he reassured me. "I'm good as new." To illustrate the point, he sat up and lifted up his blood-stained T-shirt. The gaping wound that'd caused all the chaos was gone.

I wondered why his blood ate through flesh and not clothing... Curious.

"I didn't hurt you, did I?" he asked with a frown.

I held up my hands and shook my head. "All fixed, see?"

Jackson took them in his own and inspected my palms. "How did you do that?"

"I don't know. I'm not asking any questions, either."

"Which translates to you don't want to ask because you're afraid of the answer."

"You know me too well," I drawled, tugging my hands out of his grasp. Sitting up, I rubbed at the sleep in my eyes.

"If you're done playing touchy-feely, we've got shit to do," Wilder declared, striding into the room.

"Good morning to you, too," I declared.

"It's evening already," he corrected. "About six p.m. We need to synchronise watches."

"It's six o'clock?" I exclaimed. "Seriously?"

"You zapped yourself pretty hard," Wilder said. "Sleep is good. You'll need a full battery tonight."

Wiggling his eyebrows, Jackson stage-whispered, "He's got a plan."

"I have a contact in the city who's good at getting around things," he confirmed. "Darkness, Light, that kind of thing."

"Why are you just pulling out this card now?" I grumbled, still half-asleep. "We could've used it *last night*." His muscles were bulging out of his tight T-shirt and it only gave me awkward memories of sharing a mattress with him last night. It didn't help that he looked fresh as a daisy, either.

"Because you never go for the nuclear option when there might be a subtler approach."

"He's right," Jackson said. "In Call of Duty—"

"This isn't one of your gamer geek tournaments," Wilder interrupted with a scowl.

"Thanks, but I already had the reminder hammered into me last night."

I snorted, proud that Jackson was standing his ground. He was too good-natured sometimes and Wilder had been walking all over him because of it.

"So what's the nuclear option?" I asked, bringing the subject back onto topic before it derailed entirely. "And why haven't you mentioned this contact before?"

Wilder sighed, clearly frustrated. "Because she's secretive, dangerous, and irritating as hell."

"Has he got a woman in every port?" Jackson asked.

"Trust me, you don't want this one in your port."

"*Gross*," I hissed. "Where are we going?"

"Covent Garden," Wilder replied, sliding on his leather jacket. "You want some dinosaur spaghetti before we go?"

**14**

———

Wilder taught me how to weave a cloak as we waited for the tube at Manor House station.

Tucked at the end of the platform, his crash course was quite effective at rendering all three of us invisible to the handful of humans waiting with us. As the train rushed out of the tunnel, we were buffeted by a blast of hot air that had a metallic tang to it. So far, so good, but we were about to ride into the belly of the beast.

Who knew what was going to happen.

Wilder was tight-lipped about his contact, which could only mean it was something I wasn't going to like.

When we got off the tube at Covent Garden, we made our way off the platform, following the exit signs.

"I'm getting a hit," Jackson said, tugging on the hem of my jacket.

"Where?" Wilder asked. "Which direction?"

"Behind us. Not far. About three or four meters. I think it was on the train."

"They're pulling out all the stops," I said. "I didn't feel anything."

"Neither did I," Wilder admitted.

We kept walking, trying not to alert our shadow that it'd been made. We climbed a set of stairs and turned down another tunnel, following the mass of commuters tracking towards the exit.

My Light began to flare inside me and I knew something was behind us. I knew this creature. I'd fought one before on the streets of Moorgate. It had a human form but could twist its body into something grotesque and deadly.

"Lesser demon," I murmured, turning my head slightly.

"We're cloaked, but don't draw your arondight blade unless you have to," Wilder warned.

"We need to kill it," I hissed.

"Yeah, but quietly." He shot me a warning glance. "Remember your training, Purples. We fight for the Light in the shadows." He was giving me the first strike.

Not wanting to let Wilder down, I shortened my stride, mentally checking for my weapons. Cold iron dagger in my boot. Arondight blade in my inside jacket pocket. I had to catch it in case we could pry information out of it. It was a long shot, but intel was intel when you were on the run.

One, two, *three*. I turned, using my Light to rush towards the spot I sensed the lesser demon lurking.

My gaze met the silver reflection of a man four paces behind us. To everyone around him, he looked just like every other suit commuting after a day at the office, but one look told me the illusion was only skin deep.

Casting a cloak over the demon, I took a step towards it, but the demon let out a deep, animalistic growl when it realised it'd been made. It leapt into the air, pushing off the side of the tunnel and started to run upside down along the roof.

"That's new," Jackson said.

"We've got to stop it before it betrays our position," Wilder said. "Try to keep up."

He took off down the tunnel after the demon, weaving and dodging the fast-moving flow of passengers. Jackson and I followed, leaping and twisting our own path of pursuit.

We emerged from the tunnel into the main concourse of the station and the demon suddenly doubled back, vaulting over Wilder, barrelling straight for me. Jackson leapt at it, forcing it to stumble and almost crash into a group of women walking towards the escalators, but I was there to grab it.

I fisted my hands into the front of its shirt and forced it back into the wall. Wilder opened a random door and I twisted, forcing the demon into the room beyond. Jackson slipped through the gap, then Wilder closed us into the darkness.

"*Arondight*," the demon moaned, its breath stinking like rotting flesh.

"Be careful what you wish for," I said as Light lit

up the room. It was an office of some kind, luckily closed down for the night. "Where is he?"

"Pretty purple." It opened its mouth in a twisted grin, revealing rows of dirty, rotting teeth.

"*Dude*," Jackson exclaimed, "it stinks."

"Demon," it chortled. "Pretty demon. Human demon!"

"Shut the hell up and tell us where the Balan is," Wilder said, pressing the edge of his cold iron dagger against the creature's cheek. Flesh sizzled, and it cried out in pain, the sound grating in my ears.

Its eyes rolled and its limbs began to twitch. "*Up your arse.*"

The sound of breaking bones tore through the air and I pushed away from the demon as it began to change. Wilder flipped his cold iron dagger in his hand and slammed it into the creature's chest. It wailed and thrashed against the power pinning it in place.

Remembering my training, I reached for my arondight blade and willed it to life. Violet sparks showered across the room and I struck with deadly precision.

The demon shuddered, its mouth gaping open, and burst into flames. In a *whoosh* of heat that lasted barely two seconds, it was swallowed whole, then gone completely.

Jackson stared at the scorch mark on the ground as I sheathed my blade. I hadn't killed a demon like that since that night in Moorgate, and even though I now knew what I was doing, it didn't make it any easier. After all, it did have a human face.

"I'll never get used to seeing that," Jackson said, echoing my thoughts.

"Good," Wilder said, slipping his dagger back into his boot. "The day you start liking it is the day you've crossed the line."

"He wasn't going to tell us anything," I said. "I don't know why you tried."

"You never know." Wilder glanced at Jackson, who was scuffing the toe of his boot across the black mark on the floor. "They're not all cannon fodder. Some demons actually *value* their lives."

I rolled my eyes, slipping my hilt into the inside pocket of my leather jacket. "Let's get out of here."

We slipped back into the tunnel and climbed the escalator to the surface. When we reached the top, we leapt over the barriers and breathed in the cool, clear outside air.

"You guys must save a heap on tube fare," Jackson said.

"It's not like we can deduct it as a work expense on our tax return," Wilder replied dryly.

He led us down the street, away from the marketplace, and we emerged out onto a busy crossroads.

Seven streets converged into one confusing roundabout with cars and people going in all directions. Tourists snapped photos on their mobile phones of the tall column in the middle of the chaos, and people came and went out of the various restaurants and cafés.

The more I studied each offshoot of the dial, the dizzier I became. I could see how people got turned around in this intersection. If you didn't know where you were going, you could end up anywhere. That was a metaphor if I ever heard one.

"This is Seven Dials," Jackson said. "I read about it online."

Wilder snorted. "You live in London and you've never been here before?"

"You could live here for a thousand years and never find all its secrets," he shot back.

"You need to get out more—"

"And we need to get off the street," I interrupted. "I don't want to have another public fisticuffs if I don't have to, *thank you very much*."

"Be careful you don't bump into anyone," Wilder said just as my shoulder collided with a man who was walking past. The guy looked up for someone to apologise to but ended up scratching his head in confusion.

Ignoring my scowl, Wilder led us along the northern dial, then turned sharply to the right. The alley was narrow and the cobbles were slick from millions of footsteps. It was only wide enough for two people to walk abreast, so dodging oncoming traffic was almost impossible. Brick buildings rose two- to three-stories above us, casting imposing shadows, but lights and boutique shops and cafés lit the way. The scents of organic skincare products, coffee, food, and perfume filled the crisp winter evening air as we emerged into a little courtyard packed full of folding tables and chairs.

The din was bordering on noise complaint levels, and music ebbed out of the teeny pub on the corner. Sometimes, London never failed to surprise me with the treasures in its hidden corners.

Bristling at the amount of people who were lingering, I glanced around, but couldn't sense any demons. It was like they were avoiding this place.

Wilder pointed to the top floor of the building in front of us. "There."

I looked up and wasn't sure what I was looking for. The window trims were painted in bright colours, and planter boxes were full of greenery spilling down over the sides like a makeshift English cottage jungle. Above us, fairy lights twinkled. It was all sweet and magical, and nothing like I'd expected.

"Where?" I asked, spotting a rooftop garden peeking over the façade. "Am I missing something or does your contact live in the hipster hippy mecca of Covent Garden? The rent must be epic."

Wilder sighed and place his hand on my shoulder. "Look *harder*."

I felt his Light stir and the façade shimmered, revealing a narrow house jammed between the skincare shop and the vegan bakery. I shook my head, my Light tingling as the illusion gathered us into its arms. It wasn't even funny how much I still had to learn about this world.

"It's in the middle of one of the busiest parts of

London," Jackson said, revealing that he saw it too. "How doesn't anyone see it?"

"How doesn't anyone see us?" Wilder asked, raising an eyebrow.

"Point."

"Can you feel it?" Wilder asked me.

I nodded. "Shadows aren't allowed here."

"What about me?" Jackson swallowed and shook his head. "It's hard to know where I'm classified as Dark or where I can get away with being Light."

"Don't worry." Wilder smiled and slapped him on the shoulder. "If she didn't want you here, you'd know about it."

Jackson looked at me and made a face. "And that fills me with so much confidence."

"How did you reveal it?" I asked, glancing up at Wilder.

"Lesson number two when using your Light—you need to see past the surface. Illusion is only a thin veil."

That was why his house wasn't one hundred percent invisible to the Naturals. The thick cloak he'd built up made it difficult, but if someone knew what to look for, the illusion would shatter. But only for them and those the cloak itself invited.

"I need to learn how to call upon my Light and how to use it with intent."

Wilder smirked. "Aw, you do listen."

He didn't wait for an answer. He strode towards the house and the door creaked inwards, opening on its own in a clear invitation.

Shrugging, I followed him inside with Jackson right behind me.

Immediately, I felt heat press against my cheeks. Warmth radiated through the air, stirring the plants, moss, and lichen that were growing out of every nook and cranny their roots could take hold in. A thorny rose bush billowed out of the fireplace, growing crimson blossoms like something out of *Beauty and the Beast*. Vines and creepers twisted up the staircase, completely encasing the bannister. A thorny bush with pink flowers nestled over the coffee table. Wisteria draped from the ceiling, its thick, woody trunk propping up the entire second floor.

"Wow," I whispered.

"She likes plants," Wilder stated.

We weren't the only living things that were lingering in the house. The corners were spun with the silky gossamer strands of multiple spiderwebs, only adding to the spooky hunted-forest-inside-a-house vibe.

"It's creepy in here," Jackson whispered.

Where the hell had Wilder brought us? I shivered, the feeling we were being watched intensifying.

"Who is this contact exactly?" I asked, my nerves on edge.

"She's a druidess," Wilder replied. Turning to the corner, he smiled. "One of the last. Isn't that right?"

A figure melted out of the shadows—a woman, gnarled by time with her hunched back and knobbly fingers.

"Special, I am," she purred, her eyes flashing.

She looked like any other sweet grandmother with her slacks, slip-on shoes, hand-knitted jumper, and permed snowy hair, but after Wilder had just schooled me on illusion, I knew there was more to her than met the eye. Her crooked back and frail frame concealed something a lot more ancient than eighty human years.

I could feel the power swirl in the woman's bones and I glanced at Wilder, my nerves beginning to tingle. I hadn't even sensed her, but now that she was revealed, I understood why the demons were leaving this place alone.

"Druidess, like Druids?" Jackson asked. "Like Merlin?"

"Merlin, *pah!*" the woman exclaimed, spitting on the floor.

Jackson took a step back out of the blast radius. "Not a friend of yours, then?"

"You know why we're here," Wilder said. "You've felt the Darkness stir over the city."

"Seven obscure passages. Seven different roads. A place for the less fortunate to find their fate," she said cryptically.

"Does she always talk like that?" I asked.

"Words have power," the druidess said, her gnarled hand slapping me upside of the head. "You best listen, girl."

"Ow!" I exclaimed, rubbing at the sting.

She glared at me, her eyes flashing with a strange holographic rainbow. "They're looking."

"So are we," Wilder said, leaning against the

fireplace. He picked at the moss growing between the brickwork. "I like what you've done to the place. Eglantine this time?"

The druidess smiled, clearly pleased. "Sweet-Brier." Turning to a thick mess of thorns and pink flowers, she plucked one and thrust it at me.

I smelt the blossom and made a face. "Mmm. Smells like apples." Clearly, the woman liked growing things. Maybe affinity with nature was the Druid's power?

"You want something?" she asked Wilder after thrusting another flower into Jackson's hands. "Dark the night is, boy."

"We're looking for a demon."

She scowled and waved her hand at him. "Lots outside. *Look*."

"We're interested in one in particular. The Balan demon who attacked the Sanctum."

The druidess pouted and shuffled across the room agitated. "Stupid boy. Too much."

I went to open my mouth, but Wilder held up his hand to silence me. "What is it this time? Seeds for your garden? Sweets? I know you like Galaxy chocolate."

I looked at Jackson, who was watching the exchange with amusement. Was Wilder *flirting* with her?

She shook her head. "No Galaxy. They have something I want. I need."

"Do you want it, or do you need it?" Wilder asked. "They're two very different things."

"Want and need are irrelevant. You get, I find."

"She drives a hard bargain," Jackson said. "Where were you when I needed someone to negotiate my sponsorship contracts?"

The druidess turned to him, her gaze raking up and down. After a while, she seemed satisfied with what she saw. "Interesting."

He shrugged. "Uh, thanks?"

"You've got competition, Purples," Wilder drawled.

I fired him a warning glare. "*Shut up.*"

"Greater demon," the druidess said with a shake of her head, "too much."

"We know he's powerful, otherwise we would have found him already," Wilder replied. "Don't worry about me. You know I always hold up my end of the bargain." He held out his hands and gestured for her to take them. "Show me what you want. I have help this time."

The druidess slid her weathered hands into his and her eyes flashed. I felt a surge of power flow into Wilder and readied myself, but he didn't flinch.

"See?" she asked. "Find?"

His lips quirked and he opened his eyes. "It'll be tough, but anything for you."

"Good boy." She grinned at Jackson and beckoned him closer. "Collateral."

"You want me to stay here as a safety deposit?" Jackson's mouth fell open. "*Nah ah.*"

"I'm old, not stupid," she stated. "You get. I find. I give back."

"You'll be fine," Wilder said, rolling his eyes. "We'll be back before you know it."

I wasn't entirely sure about that. We were about to go out into a city crawling with demons and Naturals searching for us, but *no biggie*. I grimaced, but what choice did we have? I mean, the druidess could just tell us where the Balan was, but whatever she would tell us must be important enough to want collateral to make sure that Wilder held up his end of the bargain.

Wilder smiled at her. "We'll return before sunup."

The druidess nodded, then looked at me. Her gaze was haunting and slashed right through my soul.

I got the feeling she knew something about me I wasn't seeing. I was sure she'd have a high price tag on it, but I couldn't shake the sensation.

"Go," the druidess said. "You'll find."

The number thirty-eight bus rolled along the empty streets as it moved away from central London.

Peering out the window, I watched the city flash by. I wondered what was so important to the druidess that she needed to keep Jackson as collateral. It wasn't like we weren't going back anyway.

Wilder pressed the button on the pole and the bell rang, signalling the driver for the next stop.

"What's so important about Hackney?" I asked, watching as we went by the train station. It seemed the most unlikely place for demon shenanigans there was.

"She wants some runes," Wilder told me.

"Runes?"

"Druidic runes," he replied. "They're difficult to make and at her age, she's not up for it. They're extremely rare these days. To be honest, I've never seen one before. She knows where they are but won't go get them herself."

"Why not? I could feel her power. Especially when she smacked me on the back of the head."

"Which was hilarious, by the way."

"Thanks for the sympathy."

"She has agoraphobia," he explained. "Centuries of persecution will do that to a person. I get her things and she helps me in return." It was sweet in a way. She was the closest thing to a grandmother Wilder had. "She trusts me, and you don't take the trust of a druidess lightly."

"She sounded like Yoda," I quipped. "What's up with that?"

"English was never her strong suit. Language was different in her time."

"Does she have a name?"

"I'm sure she does, but in her world, names have power."

The bus came to a stop and the doors squealed open. Stepping out into the night, I flipped up the collar of my jacket and scanned the street. Nothing stirred apart from the bus behind us. The doors closed, then it moved back out onto the road and continued along the route.

We stood on the footpath, watching the red double-decker grow smaller and smaller until it turned a corner and finally disappeared.

"Will Jackson be all right?" I asked. "She won't hurt him, will she?"

"No. Not unless we try to double cross her."

"I wonder what she wants with him?"

Wilder snorted and shook his head. "She's a thousand-year-old crone who's afraid to leave her invisible house. What do you think?"

Tea and biscuits. *Obviously.*

"Did you ever wonder if you're descended from the Druids?" I asked.

"What makes you ask that?"

"Her eyes had a rainbow sheen when the light caught them."

He shook his head. "The last of the Druids were killed in the weeks after the cataclysm. It isn't possible."

"Then who was that we just spoke to, huh?"

"She's supposed to be dead, like the rest."

I sighed. "Have you ever heard of dormant genes?"

"Thanks for the science lesson, Purples, but every avenue was explored a long time ago. I'm an anomaly."

"The next stage in Natural evolution."

"Let's not get ahead of ourselves." He looked up and down the street, sniffed the air, then started walking.

I followed him, my mind racing. Even if we were able to find and defeat the Balan, Wainthrope wouldn't make our return easy. We'd broken about a zillion Natural laws getting Jackson out of the Sanctum. I didn't really know how the Naturals punished their criminals, but with all the Light, swords, and scary demons flying around, I imagined some pretty gruesome things.

I wondered what Greer, Aldrich, and the others were doing. If they were safe, if they were out thwarting the search, or working to overthrow the Inquisitor's corrupt hold on the Regula. I hoped it was all three.

We crossed the road and went under the rail bridge. A large expanse of open greenery surrounded by a low metal fence was on the other side. A sign told us this was Hackney Downs.

As we moved through the gates and stepped onto the springy heath underfoot, I shivered. Winter was pretty bearable in the city, but at this time of night, I could feel the ice get sucked into my lungs with every breath I took. An odd stillness had settled over the parkland, the orange lights of the suburbs beyond barely making a ripple.

It was like nothing lived here at all. Not even the usual mangey grey foxes were pulling rubbish from the bins in their night-time scavenging.

I tugged on Wilder's sleeve. "Can you feel that?"

He nodded. "We're in demon territory."

So that's what that was. It didn't sound, or *feel*, good. Agoraphobic or not, it was no wonder the druidess didn't want to get the runes herself.

Visions of a horde of inky black creatures swarming us filled my mind and I shifted uneasily. "Let's just get the runes and get out of here. I don't like being so exposed."

Wilder nodded and led the way across the park.

Our footsteps were muffled as we walked on the springy heath.

We passed a pair of tennis courts and a playground, both standing eerily silent. What was it about an adventure playground at night that made it so creepy? The weight of my arondight blade in my inside pocket was a comfort as it pressed against my side.

Continuing out across the meadow, we crossed over a cricket pitch before Wilder stopped and waved his hand through the air.

The air shimmered slightly as if I was staring at a mirage on the horizon on a hot day. When it cleared, it revealed a hidden pair of heavy metal doors set flat into the ground. I sensed the cloak still lingering and glanced over my shoulder. It wasn't anything cast by a Natural.

"This is it," Wilder said. "Exactly where she said it'd be."

"What is this place?"

"An underground something-or-rather. A bunker of some kind. She really wasn't sure."

I snorted. "A secret bunker underneath Hackney Downs. Do you know how absurd that sounds?"

"Kind of like demons and magical powers and invisible demon hunters," Wilder declared.

I watched on as he secured and opened the door, too apprehensive about what we'd find inside to think of a good comeback. Other than a few steps down into the earth, I couldn't see much at all. Once Wilder seemed satisfied there were no threats in the immediate vicinity, he led the way down into the unknown.

The moment I passed the threshold, it was as if someone had sucked out all the light and warmth from the air—not that there's been much of either to begin with. It was completely and utterly dark.

I tentatively cast out my Light, using it to guide my way.

Our footsteps echoed off the concrete as we descended a flight of stairs. I counted twenty before it turned and went down another twenty. By the time I got to a hundred and forty, we'd reached the bottom, and Hackney Downs—and the rest of London—was far overhead.

It felt old and musty down here, damp and cold. Maybe this place had been one of those old World War II air-raid shelters in a past life. Abandoned and forgotten by humanity, demons had taken it over.

"Wait," Wilder murmured, his voice loud in the enclosed space.

I lingered behind him, using my Light to sense what was in front of us—a large door edged in inky blackness.

"There're alarms," he said. "Hang on." I sensed his Light stir and a moment later, a high-pitched whine tore through my ear drums.

Slapping my hands over my ears, I cursed. "What the hell is that?"

"The security system overloading."

I shook my head as the sound from the alarm cut off, my bones still vibrating. The door creaked open, letting light back into the dark. I blinked, dazed, even though the hallway beyond was in near darkness itself. Listening to the silence, it was too still to be natural. Something didn't feel right…

When I heard a soft twang, I gasped. "*Wi*—"

Wilder had heard it too. His hand shot up into the air, faster than I thought possible, and grasped the shaft of an arrow that'd fired out of the darkness. The tip was barbed and dripped with Darkness and I moved back a step.

"A trap." Snapping the arrow in half, he raised an eyebrow. "Watch your step, Purples. You don't want to end up as a shish kabob."

I shuddered and moved around the trap, stepping farther into the shadows. Talk about on-the-job training.

Wilder found a trip wire at the end of the hall. He leaned into the room beyond, checking what it was attached to.

"More Darkness," he said. "Demons definitely live here."

"They're not at home," I murmured, conscious of the way the air didn't move. Not even our breath stirred a slight breeze. "I can't sense anything."

Wilder grunted and stepped over the wire. "This trap smells like your man-toy."

Once I was in the room, he knelt down and disarmed the wire so we wouldn't trip it on the way out.

I sniffed the air. "It smells like…antiseptic and medicine."

"Genetically altered Darkness," Wilder said cryptically.

Turning, I found a light switch and flicked it on.

"Uh, I think you're right," I said, staring at the hidden bunker the druidess had led us to.

It was a laboratory.

Stainless steel counters ran the length of the room, their surfaces littered with microscopes, autoclaves, tools, computers, and paperwork. At various intervals were glass-fronted refrigerators lit from the inside out. Vials, petri dishes, and test tubes were stacked inside, each containing various liquids, including what looked like blood samples.

I picked up a file on the bench in front of us and flipped through the contents. The numbers and graphs didn't mean much to me, but I recognised the project name printed at the top of each page.

Wilder saw it too and took the file from me.

"Scarlett…"

*Human Convergence Project - Beta Site.*

"The Balan demon," I said. "Human Convergence is his pet project, isn't it? This is his work."

"Don't get too excited," Wilder said. "This could merely be an outpost. It says *Beta Site*. Beta as in second. It doesn't look like that have the equipment to do much of anything but some research and testing."

"Yeah, but if we get him, we get the whole thing. We can end it, and I can get revenge for my parents. Wilder…I could find out who they were."

"But we don't know the Balan demon is behind this for sure," he said.

I didn't need any more proof to convince me, though. Everything that'd happened had always led back to the Balan. Jackson's mutation, their desire to find me, the incursion at the Sanctum, Greer and her past involvement in the project, and then there was the bit where the Balan had drilled into my mind and tried to trick me into selling him my soul. This had his greasy fingerprints all over it.

Then there was the druidess. She knew who we were looking for, but who's side was she really on.

"She knew, didn't she?" I asked. "She deliberately asked for the runes because she knew it'd lead us here."

"Probably."

"Then why didn't she say? If she wanted something that was in a place we've been looking for…" I shook my head.

"It's not the way Druids do things," Wilder explained. "They like riddles and mysteries and teaching lessons to creatures lower than them."

"Wow. Sounds like my mentor."

He snorted. "She knew the answer but wanted us to work for it. The lesson is in the doing, not the result."

"Sounds like something I read in some Codex."

"We need to find the runes before a horde of angry demons come rushing in," Wilder said, changing the subject.

"Is this really about some fancy runes?" I complained.

"Yes, she really wants them, Purples." He pointed to the right side of the lab. "You start on that side."

"If you've never seen a rune before, how do you know what we're looking for?"

Wilder shook the handle on a drawer under the desk beside him, but it was stuck. "She showed me."

I stared at him, waiting. "Well, are you going to show *me*?"

"Rocks, Purples…" he said. "They look like rocks."

I snorted and turned to the laboratory. We came all this way, risked death by Darkness booby trap, for some rocks?

Running my fingers over the stainless-steel bench, I studied a refrigerator full of blood samples. Long, white labels were wrapped around each with various numbers and codes written on them. Each shelf belonged to a sequence. What they were for, was anyone's guess.

Tilting my head to the side, I realised the blood samples in the test tubes were all labelled with names, most likely from their test subjects—Anderson, W. Ballinger, A. Webb, J.

Jackson Webb. *Our Jackson.*

"They've got Jackson's blood samples," I exclaimed, wrenching open the fridge. The vials clattered as I took out the stand.

"What?" Wilder was next to me in an instant.

"That's impossible. The demons never had contact with him."

"He got cut up last night," I argued. "He was bleeding pretty heavily. Could they have gotten samples then?"

"Not like this…" He picked up a vial and held it up to the light.

"Then it had to be someone at the Sanctum." I didn't want to say it, but there was no other explanation. "Someone with an axe to grind. Someone like—"

"*Wainthrope*," he snarled.

"How do you know? I get he's a corrupt piece of shite, but in league with demons?"

A Natural working for the Dark was about as bad as it could get. If we were going to throw around accusations, we'd better be sure. I was totally learning not to do that whole run-head-first-into-danger thing.

"These are vials from Ramona's lab," Wilder explained. "The labels are the same. Who else do we know that'd do something like this?" He raised his eyebrows. "He wasn't going to execute Jackson, Purples. He was going to *hand him over*." Which meant he was working with the Balan demon.

"*Shite*…" I whispered, a chill passing through my heart. "I wish you still had your mobile. We could use the evidence."

"We've got the next best thing," Wilder said, tugging open my leather jacket. Reaching into the inside pocket, he took out the troll doll and sat it on the counter. In all the excitement, I'd forgotten I'd put it there.

"What good's that going to do? You better not melt the poor thing. I've gotten attached to it."

"It's the next best thing to data storage we have." He nodded towards the lab. "Keep looking. This is going to take a while…and I won't melt you, I promise."

He tapped his index finger against the troll doll and called on his Light. Its warmth seemed to lure me towards it, but I shook my head and turned back to the laboratory. I could ask him to teach me the mechanics of backing up my data to my troll doll lookalike later.

There wasn't much else to paw through as I worked my way down the length of the room. I opened another fridge, rustled around in drawers, and overturned a cardboard file box. Everywhere I looked was evidence that the demons were doing some serious testing with their biological weapon.

Jackson wasn't the only mutated human out there.

We had to warn Greer and the others, but first…

I turned, my gaze falling on a wooden box in the far corner. It wasn't like anything else in the lab, which meant it must be what we were looking for.

Sliding it across the stainless-steel counter, I ran my hand over the carved surface, feeling the energy pulse from within. I flipped open the brass latch and opened the lid. Inside, sitting on a bed of plush velvet, were three smooth rocks, each no larger than my palm.

They were nothing more than pebbles anyone could pick up from a riverbank or stream. The first was an earthy brown colour, the second was slate-grey, and the third was a creamy quartz.

Intricate symbols had been carved into each—the precise chisel marks ran deep but hadn't caused the stones to break, even though the dark grey would've shattered without much force at all. The temperature around the box seemed icier than the rest of the room as if the dormant power inside was sucking all the energy into them. *Darkness.*

"Wilder," I called out, "I've found them."

He appeared beside me, the troll doll in his hand. "That's them."

"They're made of Darkness," I said, my nose wrinkling. "What does the druidess want with these?"

"Nothing good, I'm sure."

"We can't give them to her. Aren't we honour-bound to destroy them?"

Wilder look troubled but shook his head. "We don't have a choice, Purples. This is bigger than us now. It always was, but now it's on a different scale. Wainthrope is working with the demons who killed your parents. He was going to sell out Jackson, and who knows what he would've done with you. We've got bigger fish to fry than a thousand-year-old druidess with some Darkness-infused pebbles." He snapped the lid of the box closed. "We've got what we came here for and then some. Let's go."

"Wait. We need to put a kink in the Balan's diabolical plans for world domination." I looked around for something flammable, but Wilder coughed.

"Uh, Purples…we're Naturals. We don't need chemical reactions to burn shite down."

My eyes widened. "We can do that?"

"There's a reason they leave this stuff for the advanced class," he said. "Just don't go around trying to light candles or anything, okay?"

"How do I do this?"

He grabbed my hand and slapped it down onto the counter. "Think about fire."

I made a face. "Is that it? That seems too easy."

"Don't burst all your brain cells at once, Purples. Imagine that Balan rotating on a spit."

"Okay." Flames ran across the bench and licked at the refrigerator where Jackson's blood samples sat. Easy.

Wilder tugged on my sleeve as the blaze intensified. "Hey, Purples? I think we better run."

We sprinted down the hall, heat licking at our heels. Taking the stairs two at a time, we raced for the surface. My breath tore through my lungs and my heart galloped at an alarming rate, and the surface still a long way off. The stairwell began to fill with an orange glow, pushing us to move quicker. *One hundred and forty steps…*

Finally, the glow from the city above melted through the darkness. Wilder broke the surface first and reached back for me just as a deafening boom erupted from below. The force of the blast pushed me up the last few steps, collecting Wilder on the way, and we rolled out onto the heath. Flames shot up out of the bunker opening and into the sky, the shockwave rocking the Earth before dissipating.

Checking to see if I still had my eyebrows, I breathed a sigh of relief when they were still intact. My heart pounded in my chest and adrenalin had me wired.

We lay flat on our backs, staring up at the sky. In the distance, sirens wailed like a pack of wolves howling at the moon.

I began to laugh, the manic sound echoing across the park. *What a rush.*

"You really put your back into it," Wilder quipped.

I wiped at my tears. "You got enough juice left for a cloak? I'm beat."

"After that performance, you can have all the juice you like."

**16**

———

"That was too easy," I said as we rode the bus back to Covent Garden.

Leaning his arms on the back of the seat, Wilder peered at me, his left eyebrow rising. "Don't look a gift horse in the mouth, Purples. There'll be plenty of demons to kill soon enough."

It was still a long way from sunrise when we got off the bus near the tube station. This time of the year, the nights were long and the days were barely eight hours long. The city was already stirring, the morning commute a permanent fixture no matter the time of year.

Our stride was long, both of us keen to get the runes back to the druidess. Wilder was carrying them, but even I could sense the toll they had on people like us. They sucked in Light like they were miniature blackholes.

As we rounded a corner, a tingling sensation ran down my spine. I lifted my head and scanned the

205

street. It was the same reaction I usually got when I sensed Wilder was close—in the Natural kind of way, not the inappropriate crush on your mentor kind, *thank you very much.*

I brushed my arm against Wilder's to get his attention.

"Naturals," I murmured, putting my head down. I really had to invest in a hat of some description. Wilder could blend, but my purpleness had me all kinds standing out.

"Keep walking," he replied. "Don't make any sudden movements."

In all the lessons I'd had on hunting and excising demons, no one had ever taught me how to shake a Natural tail. Until now, I suspected we were the first to have the pleasure, unless other renegades were zipped up in a redacted file some place.

"I'm letting our cloak go," he went on. "It'll expose us to everything, so keep your eyes open."

I nodded. The last thing I wanted to do was fight one of our own.

Our shield dissipated, ebbing out slowly. We couldn't keep it up because they'd sense the Light and see right through it. We may as well have a homing beacon stuck to our arses. All our tricks were useless in the face of warriors who were trained to use the same tactics against us.

It wasn't long before I saw two figures in black tactical gear farther down the street. It was official business, then—Wainthrope had given the order. I wondered if it was to kill or to capture. In light of who we were hunting, it didn't seem to matter. Part of me expected facing off with the Balan was a suicide mission, touched by Arondight or not.

Wilder and I shadowed along the footpath, using the street's natural façade as cover. We moved from darkness to alcove, hoping they didn't spot us amongst the early morning foot traffic.

As they came closer, I was able to make out more details. *Please be someone we know.* I didn't recognise the man, which meant he was one of Wainthrope's arse-kissers, but the woman…

*Romy.*

She turned her head as if she sensed me staring and our gazes crossed. My heart leapt into my throat. She hesitated for a split-second, then nodded, melting into the night and taking the other Natural with her.

I heaved a sigh of relief and Wilder urged me to hurry on.

"They haven't been compromised," I murmured. "They're safe."

"For now," Wilder replied. "We need to hustle, Purples. We're not the only ones left on this street."

I glanced over my shoulder, wondering if Romy was stalking a demon in lieu of us. Knowing she could handle herself and then some, I followed Wilder towards Seven Dials.

The door to the druidess's ramshackle house flew open as we approached. Inside, the rising light gave the greenery an odd hue—not that it wasn't already weird in here.

Jackson shot to his feet. "You sure took your

time."

"We got your runes," Wilder said, handing the box to the druidess.

"Not without some fireworks," I added, the memory of the explosion still hot against my skin.

The druidess cradled the box against her chest, grinning from ear to ear. "Good. *Good*. Waited long, I have."

"Now, your end of the bargain," Wilder said. "Where's the Balan?"

"Must find," she announced, setting the box on the ivy-encrusted coffee table. The leaves seemed to wither, and I squinted, trying to discern if I was seeing things or not.

"He is of it," she went on. "He will lead. He connects." She gestured for Jackson to sit beside her. "Come."

"I know I can connect to it, but I don't know how to find him," Jackson grumbled.

"Silly boy," the druidess slapped him on the arm, "*I find.*"

I snorted, hiding a smile behind my hand. The woman was creepy and annoying as all get out, but I found myself actually amused by her straightforwardness—as long as I wasn't on the receiving end.

She grabbed Jackson's hand and before any of us could move, she'd whipped out a knife and cut open his palm.

"Ow!" Jackson exclaimed. "What was that for?"

"Blood makes things work," she stated before she

began to chant under her breath. Forcing his hand into a fist, she angled it over the table, careful not to get any drops on her precious runes. "Squeeze."

"Yeah, Jackson," Wilder said with a snort, "*squeeze*."

"Oh, that doesn't sound perverted at all," he muttered, doing as he was told.

The druidess began to rock back and forth, her chant increasing in speed. Whatever language it was, was old and woven tightly with power. It rolled through the room and washed over me, making my stomach gurgle. When it seemed to reach a crescendo, she waved her hand over the table.

The air shimmered, revealing a map of the city.

Jackson's eyes almost popped out of his head. "This is better than the internet!"

The druidess pointed her finger at the vision. "There."

The image rippled over a location just south of the Thames, her fingertip leaving a red splotch in its wake.

"Waterloo?" Wilder asked with a frown.

"A tunnel of death," the druidess replied. "Dark, sealed…"

A tunnel of death under Waterloo station? I really wished I had a phone so I could look it up online.

"There's old train tunnels down there," Jackson blurted, sitting up straight. "Disused tracks that were part of the Underground, and some that were used to transport the dead to cemeteries. There's even one for the mail somewhere under Oxford Street."

"A train for the dead?" I shivered but considering all the things that were buried underneath London, I shouldn't—and wasn't—surprised.

"Necropolis," the druidess announced.

"Seems like a fitting place for a greater demon to sew himself back together," I declared. "The residual energy in that tunnel must be off the charts." I wasn't sure I believed in ghosts and spirits, but after the things I'd seen, I knew it was a distinct possibility.

Wilder look troubled. Ugh, I hated when he got that pinched expression on his face. His brow creased and his eyebrows almost joined in the middle. It seemed his ripped muscles also made an appearance in his forehead.

"Can you see inside?" he asked the little old lady. "Are they in the station or the tunnel?"

"Surrounded by a wall," she replied. "I can't see past. Dark."

"Shite," Wilder cursed. "That thing's probably got the entire place on lockdown. We'll never be able to get through."

"Darkness?" I asked.

He nodded. "Likely barriers and traps, not to mention Infernals and lesser demons."

"He was rebuilding his body," Jackson reminded us. "That'd make him vulnerable, right? He'd have to have a lot of protection."

"Then it means he hasn't finished yet." I glanced at Wilder, a plan forming in my mind. "If he's weakened, then we've got a chance."

The Natural shook his head. "We've got no hope

of breaking through a barrier cast by a greater demon on our own. If there were more Naturals, *maybe*, but we're shit out of luck on that front, Purples. Plus, he's underground."

"What's the ground go to do with it?"

"It's a Hell thing," Jackson replied. I shot him a look and he shrugged. "Demons are supposed to come from Hell, right?"

"An alternate plane of existence, but close enough," Wilder drawled.

I leaned against the wall. "So they get a little more juice from dark places that've seen a lot of death. Sounds like this'll be a blast."

"How can we break the barrier?" Jackson mused. "Can I mess up the signal or something?"

The druidess cackled and sipped her tea, clearly enjoying our fruitless battle panning.

"You know how to get in, don't you?" I asked, scowling at her.

Her smile widened. "I know lots of things."

"Then help us."

"Not my problem," she replied.

"What? We risked our lives getting you those runes!" I exclaimed.

"You got plenty in return, purple girl," the druidess said, sticking her nose in the air. "Blood and fire."

I threw my hands into the air "The demons are just as much of a threat to you as they are to us. Why won't you help us?"

The old woman shrugged. "You wanted to know where it was. I've told you."

"You tricked us!"

"I gave you exactly what you asked for, Natural," she declared, speaking clearly for the first time.

"She's right," Jackson said, putting his hand on my shoulder. "*You get. I find. I give back.* Remember?"

The druidess smiled. "Smart boy." She pouted and shrugged. "Demon boy, but good boy."

"I warned you," Wilder said. *Secretive, dangerous, and irritating as hell.* "You want her help, you have to make another bargain."

I rubbed my eyes, irritated that we were so close, yet so far. We knew where the Balan was, but an old woman fond of riddles and manipulation stood in our way. I couldn't tell if she was on our side or not, but I suspected the only person she gave a shite about was herself.

"Then give me something so I know you're telling the truth," I said to her. "I don't trust that you'll turn around and trick us again."

Clearly annoyed, the druidess let out a *humph*. "To break the barrier, you need one thing."

"What?"

"The demon's name."

Wilder swore under his breath.

"What?" I asked, my scowl deepening.

"Names hold great power with demons as well as the Druids," he replied. "If you know a greater demon's true name—"

"You can control its power," the druidess said matter-of-factly.

"*Great.*" I threw my hands into the air. Clearly, we weren't going to be back at the Sanctum with a greater demon's head by dinner time.

"He won't come out until his power is restored," Wilder said. "We need his name, otherwise we don't stand a chance on our own. We barely got him last time." *And even then, it was only temporary.*

I turned to the druidess and looked her over. Taking a deep breath, I pushed away my exhaustion and anger. "What do you want?"

She patted Jackson on the knee and smiled brightly. "Demon boy."

"Me?" he exclaimed, his eyes widening in panic.

"As you can tell," Wilder began, flipping his cold iron dagger over in his hand, "the purple girl is fond of that one. I also know what you're like. I get you seeds and tea bags for help hunting down the worst of the worst in the demon world, but I wasn't born yesterday. Darkness-infused runes, your knowledge of Human Convergence, your tricks and riddles..." He snorted and knelt in front of her. "He was your price all along, wasn't he?"

She smiled, clearly not intimidated by the hulking six-foot-three Natural in front of her. Wilder's lip curled, and he slammed down the dagger into the couch beside her.

The druidess jerked and let out a wail. "My final price!"

"Not if you're going to harm him," Wilder seethed.

"Really?" Jackson asked, glancing at me. "He likes me now?"

"What are you up to?" Wilder demanded. "You Druids and your schemes. You might be the last, but you're still like them despite your differences."

She leaned forwards and the room began to shake. "*Name for boy.*"

I covered my head as dirt rained down from the ceiling, wondering if I should get under a doorway. Jackson yelped and leapt behind the couch.

"I'll stay!" he cried. "I can handle whatever it is she wants with me."

"No," I snarled, "you're coming with us."

He peeked over the top of the couch and shook his head. "He's the guy who murdered your parents, Scarlett, and he tried to turn me into a demon. If this is your only chance to kill him, then I'll stay. It can't be that bad." Looking at the druidess, he declared, "We accept your price."

"Jackson!" I shrieked. "No!"

The room immediately stopped shaking as if it was the signature *and* full stop on some mystical contract.

The druidess grinned and clapped her hands together. "It is done!" She glanced between me and Wilder a few times before gesturing to me. "You will need…"

"Me?"

"Just you, purple girl."

I hesitated.

"Just let her tell you the name, Purples," Wilder said as he rose to his feet. "The deal has been done."

I made a face and knelt beside the old woman. "Just when I started to like you, you go all sphinx on me with your riddles." I glanced at Jackson. "Are you going to hurt him? Because if you trick us again—"

The druidess sighed and grabbed my jacket. Pulling me towards her, she whispered in my ear, "*Markzoth.*"

It lodged into my mind like a bullet and my eyes widened. Now I understood why creatures protected their true identities from people like us. *Names had power.*

Standing, I looked at Wilder.

He nodded and moved towards the door.

"Scarlett?" Jackson emerged from behind the couch and embraced me.

"It'll be okay," I murmured. "We'll get him, I promise." And I wasn't letting him stay here forever—the prisoner of some ancient Druid—just like we weren't going to let him rot in the vaults. I'd come back and take him *and* the runes…by force if I had to.

The old woman smirked at me, then gathered up the box, cradling it against her chest.

If there was one thing I'd learned about Druids so far, it was the fact you shouldn't trust them as far as you could throw their gnarled, sweet, little grandmother bodies.

I slipped my arms around his waist. "I'll come back for you," I whispered into his ear, "*I promise.*"

## 17

Londonwas waking up as we ventured towards
Waterloo, the encounter with the druidess still
heavy on my mind.

*Just you, purple girl.*

I couldn't help wondering if the druidess's cryptic
dishing out of greater demon names meant I'd be
facing Markzoth on my own. *Without Wilder.* A green
trainee with a penchant for reckless risk taking.
Touched by Arondight or not, I didn't know a thing
about vanquishing anything other than Infernals and
lesser demons.

"Is this what it's like?" I asked, shivering as the
wind picked up.

"What?"

"Being a Natural."

Wilder grunted, the sound reverberating down to
my very soul. He didn't have a reply, because I
already had my answer. Sacrifice, loss, and constant
struggle—that was the reality of being a Natural.

We decided—meaning Wilder ordered me—to go on foot. I was beginning to tire after our night of adventures—vanquishing demons on the tube and blowing up a secret underground laboratory would do that to a person—and I yawned.

The Thames was running swiftly as we crossed the Waterloo Bridge—the tidal river was already bustling with water taxis, tourist boats, and other vessels. Street lights were slowly switching off as we passed, and traffic—foot and motorised—was picking up as the morning commute intensified.

Wilder told me more about the Druids as we walked. It left me wondering if this was another one of his teaching moments, or if he was trying to keep my mind off the fact that the most dangerous grandma I'd ever had the pleasure of tangling with was holding Jackson prisoner.

He told me that the Druids were born out of the ancient Celtic tribes. For thousands of years, they were held in high esteem as soothsayers, priests, and magicians. They lived long lives—at least a thousand years going by the druidess' high score—and had long memories, though they seemed to become more fond of riddles and lessons the older they grew. They had their own kind of power, neither Light nor Dark, but it came with a terrible price. What it was, Wilder didn't know, but it made them loathe to use their magic, except in the most dire of circumstances.

When the Naturals rose to power—by fighting the supernatural beings that threatened humankind—they forged an alliance with the Druids. The most famous allegiance being between Merlin and the Naturals of Camelot. His presence had been recorded in stories told over and over by humanity, but the true version of events were a little more…extreme.

By the time Camelot was destroyed in the cataclysm—the part in the story where demons were finally able to walk on the Earth in vast numbers—the Druids had dwindled, and in the ashes of ruin, the demons had hunted them down to the last of their kind. The rest of that tale was still unfolding a thousand years later.

Though, where the Druids came from and where they went after death, was a mystery. Like the Naturals, their origins had been lost to time and destruction.

It was food for thought as we approached the next stage of our hunt.

Waterloo Station was teeming with activity when we finally arrived. Wilder allowed our cloak to dissipate as we moved through an alcove, subtly returning us to visibility without alerting anyone.

People walked in all directions, rushing for trains, going to work, and wherever else they had to go in such a hurry. There had to be thousands pouring in and out of the tube and overland rail station, not to mention from busses and the street.

Bodies ripe for possession.

I couldn't shake the feeling we were walking into a trap.

"Stay alert," Wilder said, bristling with the same apprehension. "There might be Naturals around."

He didn't have to remind me twice.

We moved farther into the station, searching for a shop that sold cheap pay-as-you-go phones. Digital boards listed all the incoming and departing trains in garish orange text, the ticket machines were bumper to bumper, barriers squealed as they opened and closed, and the loud speakers blared announcements over the already noisy station.

I spotted a WHSmith convenience store ahead and nudged Wilder. While he was inside, I leaned against the wall, keeping a close eye on the surrounding crowd. I could sense something askew, but it was so faint that it was hard to tell if I was imagining things. Looking at the tiled floor beneath my feet, I wondered if the tunnel the druidess pointed us to ran right under the station.

Wilder appeared beside me, box in hand, and tore into the packaging. I waited as he put the SIM card into the back and switched the phone on. The screen lit up and prompted him to set up the language, then a passcode.

"It's got two percent battery," he said just as it switched it off. "*Piece of shite.*"

"There." I nodded towards the Caffè Nero across the concourse. "I'm hungry and in need of a sugar hit. We'll be out of sight in there while it charges."

Wilder grunted and dumped everything but the phone and charger into the bin. I considered throwing up another cloak for a moment but decided against it. There were too many people hanging around and tables were in high demand. If someone tried to sit on Wilder's invisible lap, there'd be chaos.

We found temporary refuge at the back of the café. Wilder plugged the charger into an outlet and all we had to do was wait until the phone had enough juice for it to turn on.

Pilfering a ten-pound note from my mentor, I ordered some drinks, looking totally conspicuous in my black clothes, purple hair, and leather jacket. A middle-aged lady gave me some serious disapproving side-eye and I stared back, making sure she wasn't carrying an unwanted visitor. Thankfully, she was just allergic to alternative fashion. *Man, if only she knew.*

Returning to the back of the store with our order, I slipped into a chair beside Wilder and slid him his takeout cup of black tar, AKA what he thought passed for coffee. I happily sipped on my raspberry and Belgian white chocolate frappé and intermittently dipped my finger into the whipped cream heaped on top.

Wilder watched me with a strange fascination.

"What?" I asked. "Haven't you ever had a frappé before?"

"Not when they cost more than a fiver," he replied, frowning at the twenty-three pence I handed back to him. "I prefer black coffee."

I feigned throwing up, then resumed creatively ingesting my cream and chocolate frappé, otherwise known as *heaven*.

"This isn't how I expected our hunt for a greater

demon in a tunnel of death to go," I murmured keeping my voice to a bare minimum.

"What did you expect?"

"Swords, blood, and explosions…maybe a dash of magical bad-arsery thrown in for good measure." I shrugged. "Wait. How did you get ten pounds?"

"We get an allowance from the Sanctum," he replied.

"Seriously? I haven't seen evidence of any money of any kind coming in my direction." I pouted, wondering if I could lodge a claim.

"I just gave you a tenner, Purples."

"*Semantics.*"

"Trainees don't get wages. Consider it an unpaid internship."

I scoffed and checked the phone, but Wilder had already brought up some search items while we were arguing.

"Thank goodness for the internet," I proclaimed. "Praise the… Wait. What do Naturals say? Praise the Lady?"

Wilder rolled his eyes. "We don't say anything."

"That's anticlimactic." I said with an eye roll.

"Glad to see you haven't lost your sense for witty comebacks."

"It's borderline," I warned. "It's been one hell of a rollercoaster over the last few days. I can't remember the last time I slept."

"Yesterday afternoon."

I groaned and sucked on the straw in my drink, making a loud, obnoxious, slurping sound.

Wilder didn't make a peep. He was a master of ignoring all my attempts at riling him up, which was super annoying. I mean, we were literally looking to arrange a prize fight with the big bad wolf—a little laughter wouldn't go astray.

Knowing time was short, we huddled over the phone, scanning the search results. We'd already made a big bang and stirred up the hornets' nest.

"London Necropolis," I said, jabbing my finger at the screen. "She said something about a Necropolis."

"There's an old rail line that went from here to Brookwood cemetery in the southwest part of the city. They built it because of overcrowding."

I shuddered. "Too many bodies to bury?"

"You imagine living in a town with overflowing graveyards. The stench would have been terrible."

Clucking my tongue, I turned my attention back to the phone.

"It used to be an air raid shelter in the forties," I said. "It says the main station buildings were destroyed in the war, but the underground sections were untouched."

A lot of the underground stations had been used for the locals around the city during the Blitz in World War II. I imagined scared men, women, and children huddling in the darkness, listening to the sounds of bomb after bomb exploding somewhere above, wondering what they'd find when they returned to the surface. It must've been terrifying.

"The other terminus has been completely demolished above ground," Wilder added. "And the overland rail and tunnels were filled in and built over —office blocks." He snorted. "Humans tear down beauty wherever they go."

"That's a depressing conclusion," I drawled. "We aren't so different. I used to think I was one until recently, you know."

"There's every chance that the tunnels are still accessible," he went on, ignoring me. "We just need to find a way in."

"Are you sure? The rail was overland."

"Not everything is as it seems, Purples. There were some underground sections, but who knows how far they go, or how much humans remember."

He was right. There was every chance what was left of the stations and the supposed tunnels were hidden by powers beyond humanities' knowledge. Thinking about the body parts and the swirling mass of inky darkness that made up the Balan demon, it was for the best. A Frankenstein-ed corpse was the stuff nightmares were made of.

"Of course they're still down there," I declared. "You know, we should've been more specific when we asked the druidess for a location."

Wilder grunted. "The original entrance to the Necropolis is just down the street. We'll start there."

By the time we'd returned to the footpath outside Waterloo, our cloak had returned. We moved towards the spot on the map, invisible to human eyes.

*London Necropolis.* It sounded like a really cool name for a goth club if you asked me. Wainthrope would fit right in with all the posers in their flashy

PVC corsets. I snorted, wondering what we were going to do about *him*.

The map marker wasn't far from the main station, so we found it rather quickly. We stared up at the building and compared it to the picture on the phone.

"This is it," Wilder said.

"It doesn't look like much…"

"All the original buildings were destroyed, remember? This is all that survived."

My brow creased as I studied what was left of the hub that transported London's dead to the outer reaches of the city. On the ground floor was an old office or ticket booth, then a large wrought-iron gate barred the entrance to a courtyard beyond. Over the archway, the structure rose another three stories.

The druidess said knowing the Balan's name would help us get past the barrier that was protecting this place. I wondered how I was supposed to use it…

Markzoth. Seriously, who named their kid Markzoth? Poor guy.

As if I'd willed it, the façade shimmered, revealing what was hidden from human eyes. A sign from the original building concealed underneath the supposed modern restoration—*Necropolis Station.*

"Wilder." I pulled at his sleeve, my gaze fixed on the signage.

"Shite," he said. "No wonder all those scouting teams never found where the Balan was hiding."

I could sense more within the courtyard. "Not all of it's gone." It was hidden by Darkness, which was why humans thought it was all boarded up and filled in. "That illusion was thick—"

"You know his name. That's why you can unveil it."

"It can't be that easy," I said with a shake of my head, "can it?"

"No, it's not. This is just the surface. The real fight is below."

I tensed. "I like to think I have an edge being a little purple and everything, but we can't take on a whole horde of demons on our own."

"We can't wait for back up, Scarlett," Wilder said. "The longer we wait, the more powerful he gets." He began typing a message on the burner phone. "I'll put the call in, but like I said, we can't hang around."

"What if they don't get the message in time?"

"They'll be here," he reassured me. "They'll hold the rear, while we go for the prize. We do have these protocols for a reason."

"Wainthrope knows them."

"Erm..." Wilder shifted from foot to foot and coughed.

My cheeks reddened as I realised it wasn't a Natural protocol he'd just activated, but the secret booty call code he'd used with Greer. *Awkward.*

I held up my hand and scowled. "I don't want to know the details."

Striding forwards, I pushed open the gates and moved into the inner courtyard. There had to be an access point around here some place.

A sickly stench wafted up my nose as Wilder

joined me, but something told me it wasn't his manly musk curdling past its use by date. No, this was the sweet scent of rotting flesh.

Movement drew my gaze to the shadows where I saw a creature lingering. It used to be a person, but the parasite inside them had twisted their body into a decaying mass of putridness.

Resisting the urge to throw up, I took out my arondight blade. At least we were in the right place.

"Hello," I said, "fancy seeing you here."

The creature tilted its head to the side and clicked its tongue.

I tightened my grip around my arondight blade. "I believe you know where my buddy, Barry the Balan, is."

"That's a lot of B's," Wilder said.

I arched my brow at him. "Say that ten times fast."

"Bloody Barry, the Boring Balan. Bloody Blarry, the Bloring Bllahn."

I grimaced. "I'd stop while you're ahead."

"*Naturals*," the demon hissed, moving out into the light.

It skittered across the asphalt, its knee and elbow joints bent at odd angles. Stringy brown hair hung limply from its scalp and it made this gross, yet oddly comical, squelching sound as it advanced.

I'd never get used to seeing a lesser demon in the rotting flesh. I mean, it left bits of itself everywhere it went. Sharing was caring, but there was a point where it went a little too far.

"I'm not in the mood to make any more bargains," I said to Wilder. "Negotiating sucks."

"Then you know what to do, Purples. We're not here on a diplomatic mission."

Knowing we'd get nothing out of the mindless thing, I willed my blade to life. Violet sparks rained across the asphalt, reflecting in the silver of the demon's eyes.

"Arondight?" it exclaimed, its rotting mouth falling open.

"Just a touch," I declared, advancing on its position.

The demon hissed, then leapt into the air. I pushed off the ground, using a burst of Light to propel me towards the enemy. My arondight blade sparked, showering the courtyard with indigo flame, then I struck, severing sinew and bone like butter.

I landed lithely as the demon disappeared in a hot flash of flame.

Sheathing my blade, I glanced at Wilder, and he nodded once.

*The hunt had begun.*

**18**

———

W e found the entrance to the Necropolis at the rear of the courtyard.

The complex still sat above ground, so we entered on street level through a boarded-up set of Victorian-era double doors. Leading down from the foyer was a stone staircase with an ornate balustrade.

Wilder and I descended into the shadows, both of us poised for anything that might be lurking. Where there was one demon, there'd be more.

I placed each foot down carefully as I went—heel first, then toe—to minimise noise. The air was so close, even my heartbeat sounded deafening. Surely something somewhere could hear it echo and pounce.

At the bottom of the staircase, the complex opened up into a grand reception hall. The floor was some kind of cream polished terrazzo with elaborate flourishes in the corners, though I wasn't an expert on this kind of stuff. Antique hunting at flea markets wasn't exactly my favourite pastime.

In the centre of the floor, there seemed to be a logo of some kind—perhaps of the Necropolis railway. When I looked up, I was surprised to find the roof was inlaid with stained glass, though the shards of colours were covered with grime, soot, and whatever had been built over the top. For all intents and purposes, we were now underground.

"It's still here," I murmured, awestruck at how such a large space could be hidden from the world.

It made me wonder how many mysteries could be solved with the help of a name and a little Light. Who really built the pyramids, aliens or the ancient Egyptians? Where did things go in the Bermuda Triangle? Was El Dorado really hidden in the Amazon jungle? What happened to the Mayans? Was Atlantis a real place? The list went on…

"This is some powerful Darkness," Wilder whispered. "Be alert, Scarlett."

We moved down the staircase and into the hall. Another room opened up through a doorway to the right, though it was shrouded in shadow.

At its height, the Necropolis had to have been a major operation down here. Mortuaries, places for funerals for different social classes, morgues, stockrooms, then the train platforms themselves, all built under and amongst the bustling city. It was a morbid curiosity, building a specialised railway to transport the dead to the outer reaches of London.

As we moved deeper into the dank tomb, the echo of death and transitory life grew stronger. It was seeped into every part of this forgotten place. Loss, suffering, violence, and the natural decomposition of life was the perfect petri dish for a greater demon to set up his lair.

The walls and roof were blackened with soot and fire damage charred through the walls in places. Was it from the night this place was bombed in the Blitz? Perhaps, though it was hard to tell considering demons liked to go out with a fanfare.

My boot scuffed a piece of paper and I bent over to retrieve it.

"What's that?" Wilder asked, looking over my shoulder.

"It's a programme." I turned over the leaflet and scanned the print. "For a funeral. Service, hymns, messages from the family. It's old."

"It's like a playbill at a theatre," he said with a roll of his eyes. "Humans have such weird beliefs."

"What's so weird about it?"

"Bodies are just shells for the soul," he stated.

"Well, when you put it like that…" I made a face and let the paper fall to the ground.

"I'll never understand why people need monuments. *Mary was a kind soul with three children and a cat, who made lovely scones.* Let's slap a giant arse marble angel over her paupers grave."

"Don't be so crass," I scolded him. "They're not for the dead's ego. They're a place for the people left behind, so they can visit what they lost and still feel connected."

He grunted, signalling the conversation was over, then we moved deeper into the complex.

Another set of stairs led us to one of the platforms. Unsurprisingly, it was in complete darkness, so I couldn't make out anything but the strange feeling of space, and a potential drop somewhere before me.

A cool breeze brushed against my skin—so there *was* an opening some place farther into the tunnel. Problem was, it also carried a disgusting scent with it. It wasn't like we needed any more evidence, especially when it reeked like death.

Wilder moved next to me, and I gasped as a tiny ball of Light rose from his outstretched palm.

"You know all the cool tricks," I whispered.

"Just wait until I teach you night vision."

"Night vision? Seriously? *Cool*."

"This'll do for now." He vaulted off the edge of the platform and landed on the tracks.

I followed him, my boots landing softly on one of the sleepers. There was only one way to go, southwest.

As we moved deeper into the tunnel, the stench increased and my blood whooshed faster through my veins. My skin tingled as the dull sound of footsteps echoed from the blackness before us.

*Lesser demons.*

"They're coming," Wilder whispered. "We're going to have to carve our way through the tunnel."

I swallowed hard, my hand tightening around my arondight blade.

"Remember your training, Scarlett."

"Of course." I snorted and readied myself. "I learned from the best."

"That's what I like to hear."

"If we get out of this—"

"Don't," he interrupted. "Never say that, okay?"

I swallowed hard, my thoughts going to Jackson.

"Courage, Purples." He tensed, holding out his arondight blade, "and no mercy."

Silver eyes flashed as the first wave of lesser demons ventured towards Wilder's little ball of Light. Willing my blade to life, the shadows blazed violet as the pieces snapped together in a crackle of sparks.

The demons in front began to wail, then the others joined in, the cacophony of shrieks vibrating through my entire body. Their bodies were twisted and in various stages of decomposition, but they were fast and didn't care about the vessel they inhabited. They wouldn't hold back…but neither would we.

When they leapt into range, we attacked.

I didn't think about what my sword was slicing through as I swung. All I saw was target after target. If I saw their faces, I'd either falter or throw up. Both were death sentences, so I chose not to see what was left of the humanity of their host bodies.

This was the first time I'd seen Wilder *really* fight, and I could see what all the fuss was about.

He turned, twisted, pirouetted, his blade sparking in a hypnotic pattern as he cut down everything in his path. Barely anything got past him, and when it did, I was there to finish them off. It was the first and only time I was grateful for sloppy seconds.

I lost all sense of time as we fought. The host of decaying lesser demons pressed closer, forcing us into close rage combat. I shoved away an attack with my shoulder, kicked at another, ending both with one long sweep with my blade. Indigo sparks and red flame lit the tunnel, and for a split-second, I saw the horror that awaited us…and I faltered.

A rubbery hand grasped me around the throat and I cried out as it began to squeeze. Lifting my blade, I flipped the hilt in my hand and sliced through its forearm. Immediately, the pressure eased from my neck and black blood oozed out of the creature's stump as it wailed in agony.

I gasped, sucking in lungfuls of air, then rammed my arondight blade into the demon's head. It burst into a fireball, adding scorched flesh to the rising stench.

Wilder and I fought back to back, twisting and turning, never letting the enemy break between us.

But they kept coming. Ten turned into twenty, then to thirty—two beasts appeared for every demon we vanquished.

My blade swung and slashed, and I pivoted and ducked. Everything Wilder had taught me seemed to go out the window as my life flashed before my eyes— my short and boring life, if we were being honest.

"There's too many," I cried. I was barely keeping up and my energy was starting to fail.

Wilder flipped in the air, ramming his sword through a disfigured demon.

"Hold on," he shouted. "Keep pushing."

"Wilder—" A demon collided with me and we fell to the ground in a heap. I rolled over the train tracks, pain tearing through my body, and my arondight blade was ripped out of my hand. It slid just out of reach and I scrambled, but the demon was on top of me in a flash.

"Scarlett!" Wilder let out a grunt as a demon struck him in the face.

I wrestled the creature on top of me, retching as it opened its putrid mouth. My boots pushed against the tracks in a desperate attempt to reach my hilt. My fingers scraped the metal, but I couldn't grab it before the demon snapped its jaws again.

I was locked in a desperate push and pull with life and death.

White-hot sparks erupted above us, then the demon wailed as it burst into flames. Coughing as I was covered in ash, I grasped my hilt and tensed, ready to attack, but I wasn't expecting what I saw.

*Aldrich.*

He held out his hand and hauled me to my feet.

"Am I glad to see you," I said, dusting myself off.

"Thank us later."

Another demon hurled itself at me, and I pushed back and rammed my blade through its gut. It exploded in a shower of flesh and flame. When the heat dissipated, I saw Romy, Martin, Valeria, and Alo emerge from the station in a blaze of white-hot sparks.

The horde surrounding us shrieked and wailed,

their attention divided between us and our newly formed cavalry.

The Naturals spread across the width of the tunnel and advanced into the fray, attacking with all their strength.

Valeria swirled her twin swords and sliced through a pair of demons, then Romy blew back a frenzied group with her Light, allowing Martin and Alo to cut them down. Seeing my friends all bad arse gave me the extra kick I needed for a serious comeback.

Wilder and I fought side by side, forcing the demons between us and the others. Trapping them in a pincer, we made short work of the stragglers.

Finally, nothing else emerged from the tunnel. It was a brief moment of respite to catch our breaths, because that was just a taste tester.

Wilder grabbed my arm and tugged me close. "Are you okay?"

Tensing, I nodded. I was bruised and battered, but we were alive.

"We came as quickly as we could," Aldrich said. "What's the situation?"

"The Balan is somewhere deeper in the tunnel," Wilder explained. "We didn't get far before we were swamped."

"It's him," I said, my chest heaving. "The Balan is behind Human Convergence and Wainthrope's in on it."

"What?" Martin demanded. "That's a serious accusation."

Hoping Wilder still had the troll doll, I glared at him. "We've got all the proof we need."

"*Enough*," Aldrich boomed. "Keep your focus on the task at hand, Naturals. Wainthrope will have to wait. Our primary objective is to eliminate the greater demon and clear out its lair."

"Where's Jackson?" Romy asked.

"Uh…someplace safe for now," I replied.

"How did you even get down here?" she asked, accepting my hurried explanation. "This place is *nasty*."

"And hidden by some serious demon juju," Alo stated.

"It's not on any map I've ever seen," Valeria added. "And we thought we knew all the major demon hotspots."

I glanced at Wilder who shook his head slightly. The druidess was difficult, annoying, downright unpredictable, *and* she had Jackson. Nothing good would come of me divulging our source.

"I found its name," I said. "Names have power, or so I hear."

Everyone's mouth fell open in shock, and Aldrich frowned.

Shrieks echoed from the darkness, the sound bouncing off the walls, and we turned towards the noise. With dread percolating in my stomach, I chanced a glance at Wilder and the others.

More were coming. *A lot more.*

"Go," Aldrich said. "We'll hold them off."

I shook my head. "But—"

"Scarlett. You're the only one who can put him down for good." He grasped my shoulder and gave it a reassuring squeeze. "You have his name."

"If you knew it—"

"No," he interrupted. "The more people who know, the less power it has over him."

The wails of the approaching demons intensified, and he nudged me towards the way forward.

"Go," he urged. "Be safe."

I looked to the others, but they'd already turned to face the oncoming attack.

"*Scarlett.*" Wilder grabbed my arm and dragged me down the tunnel.

I turned, gasping at the sight of a wall of Light shimmering across the breadth of the tunnel. It flared as something slammed into it from the other side, a burst of sparks showering through the barrier.

Aldrich and the others had blocked the demons from advancing. They'd closed themselves off from us, sacrificing their safety so we could complete our mission.

We were on our own. No one else was coming.

It was up to a woman with purple hair and her surly teacher to stop humanity from becoming an army of mutated super demons.

What could go wrong?

**19**

I could sense Markzoth's lair somewhere up ahead.

The tunnel was cold as the Arctic as we moved through the shadows and away from our friends fighting behind us. What we'd just faced was nothing compared to the greater demon waiting for us.

What was our edge? *Arondight.* It had to be. I was touched by the legendary sword, which hopefully meant I had an advantage when it came to fighting the bad guys. It was meant to be the thing that could end the war for good, so if I had a drop, theoretically…

An orange glow pulsed from up ahead and I glanced at Wilder. We were close.

"All that matters is the mission," he said, sensing my apprehension. "Don't worry about me. I'll back you up, but if you get the shot, you have to take it. No matter what."

"*No.*" I grabbed his hand and my Light flared, reaching out for his. "I won't leave you behind."

"We do what we must to protect humanity from the Darkness, Purples," he murmured. "Always."

"I know, but—"

"*Promise me.*"

I swallowed hard and nodded. "I promise."

He narrowed his eyes, but he squeezed my hand. The gesture was uncharacteristic, but I was glad for it. My first foray in battling demons as a full-fledged Natural had been more than I'd bargained for.

We approached the light ahead, listening for signs that someone was home. Nothing but silence greeted us, but the lingering sensation of a dark force had me on edge the entire time.

Ahead, I could see the glow ebb out of an opening that'd been blasted out of the wall and into the bedrock. Stepping through, we emerged into a cavern that'd been roughly carved into the Earth. Hunks of rock had been hacked away, creating a space for the Balan to recreate his body.

No wonder the Naturals hadn't been able to find him. This place was infused with Darkness and the coppery tang of blood.

A pile of body parts sat in the corner, the candlelight making the shadows long and grotesque.

Covering my nose with the back of my arm, I swallowed a pile of vomit. It was a confronting sight, and even though I'd expected we'd find something like this, seeing it was another thing entirely. The violence of modern TV hadn't desensitised me like I'd hoped.

A strange sigil had been chiselled into the floor and Wilder edged around it, studying the markings.

They swirled and swooped in a large circular pattern, though what it was for, I didn't know. It couldn't be anything good, considering it appeared to be filled with congealed blood.

*Ugh, it was so gross.*

Some kind of altar was at the far end of the hollow. A mess of melted red candle wax dripped from candelabras made from bone fragments and a dagger lay across the surface.

It wasn't only gross, it was creepy, too.

"I knew you'd come….*Naturals.*"

We turned at the sound of a hollow voice, both of us readying our arondight blades. He stood in the opening we'd just walked through, cold and menacing.

*Markzoth.*

He looked like an ordinary man, all signs of his Frankenstein body hidden underneath an impeccable suit and tie, but his eyes were hollow and black. Nothing shone behind them but Darkness, and the stench of pure evil rolled off him in waves. Cold, calculating, and intent on one thing—the total annihilation of the human race.

The Balan looked at Wilder and raised his hand. I felt the Darkness a split second before the demon unleashed it.

"Wilder!" I reached for him, but we were dragged apart by a blast of searing energy.

Wilder's body was wrenched into the air, his limbs flopping uselessly. Crying out, I felt his Light flare as he fought against the Balan, but it wasn't enough.

My knees collapsed underneath me and I fell in a heap on the ground, unable to move, assaulted by a blast of Darkness forced in my direction.

Wilder grunted in pain as he was flung into the air, his arondight blade skidding across the hollow. I tried to move, but my body wouldn't respond. My limbs were frozen solid, and I began to panic.

Wilder jerked and the Darkness twisted around him like a hungry snake. He was suspended as if he were hanging from a noose, the tips of his boots barely scraping the ground.

I was beginning to understand why the war between the Light and the Dark had been going on for a thousand years. We were fools to think we could face a greater demon and win. Dumb luck had allowed us to destroy his body, but now… We were in Markzoth's lair, and all the power of this place was in his control.

Crying out, I fought against the Darkness that was paralysing me. I writhed, tearing and twisting, but my body wouldn't respond. It was a strange sensation and frustrating as hell. My anger rose, hashing at the force binding me, and as it reached a crescendo, I broke free.

I brought my arondight blade to life as I flipped into the air. Swinging, I attacked with all the strength I could muster, arcing my sword through the air.

Markzoth raised his arm to block the blow, and violet sparks erupted as metal collided with corrupted flesh. He roared in anger and clamped his hand around the blade, wrenching it out of my grasp.

It fell to the ground, clattering across the rock, and the sword disappeared into the hilt.

I faltered, realising I'd done no damage to Markzoth's new body at all, and he grabbed me around the neck, his fingers biting into my skin.

"Where is Arondight?" he rasped, holding up his free hand and twisting his fingers.

"Are we still on that?" I managed to choke out. "We both know I don't know anything."

Markzoth twisted his hand and Wilder cried out in agony.

"Stop it!" I screeched, clawing at the demon's arm.

"I'm not going to stop, Scarlett," he crooned. "You're already dead. All that's left is how you choose to die. Slowly…or mercifully."

"Demons don't know the meaning of mercy," I spat.

His lips quirked and he flashed his pointed teeth. "You're right…I don't." He twirled his finger and Wilder hissed. "Where is it?"

"I don't know anything about Arondight," I rasped.

"You do, Scarlett. You know exactly where it is, and you will tell me before you die. *No matter how long it takes*."

Markzoth dragged a finger down the scar on the right side of my face and smiled. His teeth were red, the glamour holding his human form together shimmering. Rows upon rows of sharp fangs lined the inside of his mouth and I squirmed in his grasp.

"Arondight," he crooned.

My scar… Did he mean Arondight gave it to me? Was that how I'd been 'touched'?

"Pervert," I hissed.

Reaching for my Light, I forced a blast of energy towards him. His grip loosened and I was flung out of his grasp. Markzoth recovered quickly, and I shrieked in pain as his boot slammed into my ribs, the force sending me flying.

I rolled across the sigil, smearing black, congealed blood across the ground. I came to a rest near the edge, not far from where Wilder was hanging. Looking up at him, I swallowed a cry as I saw blood seep from his eyes, ears, and nose.

Wilder was cunning and powerful, second only to Aldrich, but Markzoth had rendered him useless with a flick of his demonic wrist. What hope did I have?

I clutched my side, glaring up at the demon who'd murdered my parents and had stolen Jackson's life. I hated him. I hated him so much, it almost blinded me to everything else.

"It was you who spearheaded Human Convergence, and it was you who conspired with the Inquisitor to infiltrate the Regula." I curled my lips and readied myself. "Isn't that right…*Markzoth.*"

Nothing happened. The Balan just stared down at me, flashing his rows of pointed teeth in a gleeful smile.

"Did you really think knowing my name would give you power over me?" He laughed, the sound echoing through the chamber. "*Stupid girl.*"

Ice rushed through my veins as I realised our mistake. *This was a trap.* Markzoth had seen Jackson, and everything since had been a maze of manipulation and conspiracy to get me to come to him. He wanted Arondight and since no one could find it, I was the next best thing.

"Scarlett, get out of here," Wilder managed to rasp. *"Run."*

I'd run from one thing or another my entire life— the memory of my parents' death, the abusive foster homes, myself, my struggles with mental health, and the truth of who I was. I'd finally found a place where I could belong, where I had a family and something worth fighting for.

If I ran now, I wouldn't have learned anything.

If I ran now, I'd be a coward.

If I ran now, Wilder would die.

I shook, my fingers grazing the edge of the sigil, and I called on my Light. Wilder said I could do things I wasn't supposed to. I had an instinct that protected me in battle and I healed Jackson when his Light couldn't. I was different, but we were stronger together.

*"No,"* I rose to my feet, *"I will not run."*

*"Scarlett…"* Wilder's strength was fading as mine was growing.

If I truly carried a piece of Arondight inside me, then it was time to call upon it or die trying.

I edged around the sigil, closing the gap between me and Wilder. "You don't have any power in this world, Markzoth. Not anymore."

I thrust my hand into Wilder's and let go of all the barriers I'd put up inside myself. My heart and mind opened, and his Light rushed forth to twist and mesh with mine.

A scream tore from my lips as electricity burned through my body, but it wasn't pain I felt, it was the burning acid of anger that ate through me.

"*No…*" Markzoth stared at me in shock, his glamour fading.

"Do you understand now?" I cried, a searing violet Light burning behind my eyes. *"You have no power in this world!"*

"It's—" Whatever he was about to say was lost as I unleashed the full force of my fury in a blaze of indigo flame.

The Darkness holding Markzoth and his lair together began to crack and splinter. His body tore apart, streams of inky black essence pouring out of the fissures.

Wilder's grip tightened on mine, holding me steady—he was giving me everything he had left.

I bore down on the Balan, crushing him beneath my Light, then…

He exploded in a silent vacuum of time and space, and all the light, magical and ordinary, was sucked into the void of his destruction.

---

*Scarlett…*

*Scarlett, you have to wake up. It's not over yet.*

My eyes snapped open and I gasped for air. The nothingness Markzoth had returned to had almost sucked me under. But…that voice…

I jerked upright, ash and dust falling from me in a haze that choked my throat. Coughing, I was vaguely aware Aldrich was kneeling over me.

"Scarlett?" His brow creased, and he dusted some grit from my shoulders. "Are you all right?"

I blinked, realising everyone was here—Romy, Valeria, Alo, and Martin. They were covered in foul-smelling goop, but they were alive.

"Wilder?" I rasped.

He was sitting on the ground, covered in dust, with one knee propped up. He'd attempted to wipe the blood away from his eyes, but it was smeared across his face and matted into the shaggy stubble on his jaw.

"Wilder?" I echoed.

"I'm fine," he grumbled, shaking his head.

"Your Light." I reached out, my fingertips grazing the back of his hand. When I felt his power flare in response to mine, I sighed in relief. If he'd become soul sick because of me, I wouldn't know what to do.

"What the hell is that?" Romy exclaimed, staring at the ceiling of the lair.

Following her gaze, we looked up and Alo cursed under his breath as we beheld a curious sight. Tendrils of Darkness had crawled up the walls and were working their way through the Earth towards the surface. It reminded me of a network of tree roots, except they were flowing in the wrong direction.

"What is it?" Valeria whispered. "I've never seen anything like it."

"No one has." Aldrich glanced at me and Wilder. "At least no one in living memory."

"Is that what happens when a greater demon dies?" I wondered out loud.

"Threads," Aldrich explained. "They show the connections the Balan had to the living. There was an account about it in the Codex, but I never believed I'd see it in my lifetime."

I saw the threads disappear into the ceiling like complex veins carrying Darkness to whatever they were connected to and wondered where—or to *who*—they were going to.

"The sigil," I whispered. "It was his way of controlling whoever he'd turned."

"It's leading us right to the Balan's conspirators," Aldrich confirmed.

I rubbed my temples, my head throbbing. It wasn't over, not yet. Like a bad smell that wouldn't go away, there was always a little more battle to be fought.

"Who's going to touch it?" Romy asked. "We have to find out who it was working with."

"I'm not touching that thing," Martin declared.

"Quit your whining, I'll do it." I rolled my eyes and slapped my palm down on the sigil, gasping as a vision was shoved into my mind. I wasn't surprised when I saw who the strongest thread was linked to—after all, we already suspected it, but now we had irrefutable proof.

"Julius Wainthrope," I announced. "The thread leads to Julius Wainthrope."

---

## 20

Night had well and truly fallen by the time we returned to the Sanctum in Battersea.

The stacks of the abandoned power station towered overhead, disappearing into a thick layer of fog. Snow had begun to fall, silent flakes melting on our shoulders and in our ash-laden hair.

My breath vaporised in plumes, my fingers freezing on the hilt of my arondight blade. I was exhausted, but we were against the clock. By now, Wainthrope could have taken over the whole Sanctum. Aldrich hadn't heard from Greer when he called from outside the Necropolis, and things had gone strangely silent where the demons were concerned.

A few hours ago, the city was teeming with supernaturals, but now it was empty.

"What's the plan?" Romy asked as we approached the main entrance. "Just bust in and start cracking skulls?"

"We go straight for Wainthrope," Aldrich replied, "and neutralise any hostiles in our path. We don't need any needless deaths. He must be held accountable."

"Put on trial, you mean," Martin said.

"He was one of us once," Aldrich stated.

It didn't give me a good feeling, knowing a Natural could betray the Light so completely, but it was what it was. Now we had to protect our way of life and the Codex from falling further into Darkness. If the balance tipped any more, I wasn't sure we could stop the world from falling into the hands of the enemy.

Wilder kicked in the doors and they swung inwards, crashing against the walls. A dull *boom* echoed through the marble foyer and we strode into the Sanctum like the greater demon killing bad arses we were. If we had a soundtrack in that moment, it'd be AD/DC's *Back in Black*.

Covered in demon guts, ash, soot, blood, and god knows what else, we readied our weapons as a stream of armed Naturals thundered down the stairs and out of the adjoining corridors, assuming a defensive position and cocking their automatic rifles.

"Guns?" I hissed. "Since when do we use guns?"

Wainthrope walked out onto the landing at the top of the stairs, dragging Greer behind him. *He knew.*

"What were you expecting?" he sneered down at us, hatred clouding his eyes, the statue of the Lady of the Lake towering behind him. "A parade?"

My heart twisted and I swallowed hard. He

controlled the London Sanctum and the Codex. If we didn't stop him now, then he'd take control of the Light and turn it towards Darkness. His lust for power had corrupted him to the core.

Wilder flipped his cold iron dagger in his hand and threw it at Wainthrope. It streaked through the air at an alarming pace, but the Inquisitor held up his hand, striking it down with his Light.

"Fool," he hissed. "See what they've become? They've been corrupted by Darkness! Kill the traitors!"

The Naturals cocked their weapons and began to fire, the sound deafening in the enclosed space.

I fell to the floor and scrambled behind one of the columns as bullets sprayed in my wake. Shards of stone exploded, nicking my skin as I ducked for cover. Flattening my back against the cool marble, my gaze met Wilder's. Talk about a crescendo to an over-the-top night.

The gunfire came to an abrupt halt and I looked for the others. Aldrich was pinned behind the column to my left, Wilder to the right. Romy, Martin, and Valeria had retreated outside, and Alo was in an alcove usually reserved for a bunch of wires for the electrical thing-a-mah-whatsit.

"Well, this went swimmingly," I whispered.

Wilder tapped the floor with his index finger, drawing my attention down. I tensed as I saw the thread from the Necropolis inching across the floor, past my foot, and snaking towards Greer and

Wainthrope. I had to buy some time, the thread would do the rest—or at least I hoped it would.

"Traitor!" I shouted. "You sold us all out to the demons!"

"Scarlett Ravenwood," the Inquisitor declared with a triumphant smirk, "welcome back. You're just in time for your trial."

"I think you're mistaken," I called from behind the column. "We're here to judge *you*."

"Me?" He laughed and grabbed Greer by the arm. "Shall I refresh your memory of the charges laid on you and Wilder? Not to mention Aldrich and the other defectors."

I kept one eye on the thread and one on the landing.

"No, thanks," I replied. "I don't need to be patronised by a slimy, two-faced git like you."

"*How dare you.*" The thread began to coil around his ankle, but he hadn't noticed.

"We learned a lot of interesting things while we were out and about," I went on, glancing at Wilder. "How you violated Sanctum protocol and gave Jackson's blood samples to the Balan demon." The threat grazed Wainthrope's boot. "Oh, and the part where you conspired to orchestrate his death by execution, then hand him over to the enemy. Real slick, cowboy."

"Hollow accusations from a corrupt mind," he bellowed.

"Really? Sounds like a thing a demon sympathiser would say in the midst of a tantrum." I glanced around the column just as the tendril of Darkness coiled around his ankle.

*Now!*

I lunged for the thread and wrapped my hands around it. I felt the same sensation as I had when I'd touched the sigil, but I forced it out and pulled the cord as hard as I could.

"Insolent—" Wainthrope choked and fell forwards, the thread biting into his skin.

The surrounding Naturals gasped as the thread flared, then wrapped its tendrils around Wainthrope's other leg.

Standing, I walked out from behind the column, pulling the coil of Darkness until it'd taken hold of the Inquisitor.

"He's dead," I said, dropping the thread. *"Markzoth is dead."*

His eyes widened. "You… His name—"

"Did you know when a greater demon dies, the Darkness inside it leads us to those he conspired with?" I climbed the first step. "It's quite handy, don't you agree?" I went up another step. "It tells us exactly where to cut out the corrupted flesh. And if you don't believe me, you can find it in the Codex."

The surrounding Naturals turned towards Wainthrope, their accusing glares burning like acid.

"Scarlett is right," Greer said, glaring down at the Inquisitor. "It's been hundreds of years since a sighting was recorded, but today we can write a new chapter. *The first in a century.*"

The Naturals murmured amongst themselves, and one by one, they began to drop their weapons.

The Inquisitor stared up at me with a loathing so intense the old Scarlett would've caved, but after what happened at the Necropolis, I'd evolved.

Greer moved around him and joined me. "Who will stand beside you now that they know you conspired to hand over the one man—who's single contribution to the Light *despite the Dark*—saved us all?"

The thread twisted around Wainthrope's waist, binding his arms to his sides.

"And how you planned to tear apart one of our own to further your ambitions for power?" Aldrich added.

"Don't forget the blood samples you stole from the lab and handed to the demons," I drawled.

"Your sticky fingers are all over the Human Convergence Project," Wilder said.

"Just tell us one thing, Julius…" Greer began as the thread wrapped around his chest and inched towards his neck. "Who was in control? The Balan… or you?"

The Inquisitor's eyes flickered around the foyer, searching for an ally, but he only found a wall of angry Naturals blocking his path—and a thread of Darkness so potent, it was choking the life from him.

Now I understood the truth behind the sigil. Markzoth had died, and he'd take out everyone connected with him to protect his end game from the

Light. Too bad we'd already found everything we needed to start unravelling his mutations.

"You dare defy the order of the Inquisitor?" Wainthrope exclaimed, his face reddening.

"You're only making things worse for yourself," Aldrich said.

Wilder snarled beside me and wrenched on the thread of Darkness. Wainthrope jerked and began to choke.

"I was in control," he managed to get out. "I was using *him.*"

"You can't play a demon," Wilder snapped. "Power hungry—"

I placed my hand on his arm, silencing him before got to his choice swear words.

"You think you're any better?" Wainthrope asked Greer. "Siding with a filthy hybrid and a woman who claims to have touched Arondight? You're playing with fire, Greer, and you'll get burned. Who'll save you then?"

"The old ways no longer work in this world," she said, staring down at him. "Welcome to the shadows, Mr. Wainthrope. I hope, for all our sakes, the Codex rules justly."

Aldrich brought down his arondight blade, severing the thread. As the Darkness evaporated around Wainthrope, a group of Naturals came forth and grabbed him.

"Take him to the vaults," Greer commanded.

"You'll regret this, Greer," he shouted as he was dragged away. "You'll all regret this!"

"They always fling around their empty threats when they get caught," Wilder drawled. "What a waste of breath."

Greer looked at him and moved closer. "What happened out there?"

"It's a long story."

I watched their exchange and my heart leapt with a jealous pang. Shaking my head, I rubbed my side where Markzoth had kicked me—it ached something fierce.

"Welcome home," Greer said, her gaze finding mine. "I'm sure you have an eventful story to tell, but for now, you all deserve some rest."

"And a shower," Romy declared.

Greer smiled. "That too."

I lingered as the other's began to move off, the excitement finally dying down. We'd won, but something still felt incomplete.

"Where's Jackson?" Greer asked, standing beside me.

"Someplace safe," I replied, hoping I was right. Who knew what the druidess wanted with him.

She nodded. "Understandable, but please let him know he's welcome here. I can't begin to apologise enough for Julius' actions."

"Don't apologise for him," I said. "He made his choice all on his own."

Her smile didn't reach her eyes. "Thank you, Scarlett."

I nodded and watched her move off, joining Wilder on the stairs. I was alone again. Despite everything, was that my fate? A mystery wrapped in an enigma, one too difficult to entertain, let alone love.

Aldrich moved past and patted me on the shoulder. "Don't worry about the mess," he said. "We won't make you sweep it up."

I smiled. "Thank goodness for that."

Remembering the fuss Wainthrope had made about my arondight blade, I took it out of my pocket and studied the hilt. *It wasn't a coincidence…* I didn't know where the thought had come from, but I was fast learning things happened around this place for a reason that wasn't always clear.

"Aldrich." I caught his arm. Waiting for the others to move away first, I asked, "Back at the assembly, what did Wainthrope mean when he brought up my arondight blade?"

He glanced at the others before turning back to me. "Your blade has a long history," he explained, "and a chequered one at that."

"But I was under the impression they never had an owner. The blades of the fallen are on the walls of the Sanctum."

"Those blades were retired on request of their families," he explained. "Others were too old to be reintroduced to new recruits. Arondight blades take a long time to forge and the materials have become increasingly difficult to procure. Blades have been known to be passed down through family bloodlines as well. Though, usually the unclaimed go back to the armoury."

"Then someone owned mine before," I stated. "Who?"

"That's a story for another time."

"Aldrich, please."

His forehead creased and after a moment, he took the hilt out of my hands. Turning it over, he studied every inch. It was unadorned and simple, but he seemed to see something more in its sleek design. An untold story.

After a moment, he said, "It belonged to my sister."

My heart leapt and I gasped. If it was now mine, then that meant… I swallowed hard and began to sweat.

"I'm sorry, I didn't know. If—"

"Scarlett, it's fine. Andromeda disappeared a long time ago."

"Andromeda? Like the galaxy?"

He nodded. "My parents had a thing for the letter A."

"You didn't want to retire it?"

"She wouldn't have wanted it to hang on a wall when it could be cutting down demons." Patting me on the shoulder, he smiled. "I couldn't think of a better Natural to wield her blade. She'd be honoured."

My heart warmed and I nodded. "Thanks, Aldrich."

"Go. Get Ramona to check you over and then get some rest. You deserve it."

I nodded and walked down the hall, my joints aching. I wondered how many bruises I had.

"Scarlett?"

I turned, my gaze meeting Aldrich's.

"How did you kill the Balan?"

I shrugged and ran my hand through my gritty hair. "I don't know."

It was the truth. I was inexperienced and knew next to nothing about using my Light, so whatever I'd tapped into was unknown…along with whatever link I shared with Wilder. I thought about telling Aldrich about it, but something stopped me. It felt too *intimate* to share.

Aldrich frowned but nodded, accepting my lack of explanation.

"Sleep well," he said, "Natural."

---

By the following evening, the snow had settled in every nook and cranny across London.

I always marvelled at how it insulated the most minuscule of sounds, hushing the hubbub of its eight million or so residents.

My mind was racing with more questions than answers. We'd been through so much over the past few days, and it felt as if an entire year had passed. My training, Jackson's trial, our jail break, Wilder's safehouse, the druidess, the lab…the Necropolis. So many dangers and revelations.

But most of all, I wondered about Aldrich's sister.

He'd said she'd disappeared but hadn't elaborated. It must be hard, not knowing why she never returned. I kind of understood the turmoil it caused for those left behind.

The air shifted and I huddled into my jacket and scarf. Romy had gifted the woolly purple snood to me that afternoon as an early Christmas present, and I was grateful for the warmth…and her friendship.

"Hey," I said, sensing Wilder behind me.

"Hey yourself." He sat next to me, dangling his feet over the edge of the roof.

I leaned my head against my knees and studied his profile. "Not pissed I stole your favourite brooding spot?"

His lips quirked and he shook his head. "Everything okay?"

"It's one of those endings where all the bad guys got what was coming to them but raised a whole new batch of questions without answers."

"Don't you hate those?"

"Totally."

"Welcome to the life of a Natural," he declared. "Up to the eyeballs in rotting flesh one day and untangling government conspiracies the next."

"Sounds like a binge-worthy TV show."

"How are you feeling?"

I grimaced, remembering how Markzoth had tortured him in the Necropolis. "I should be asking you that."

"Don't dent my pride, Purples. You promised me," he said wryly.

*All that matters is the mission.* His words hadn't left me, and I doubted they ever would.

I raised my eyebrows. "Is it any surprise I broke it? I do like sticking my middle finger up at authority figures."

He turned his gaze out over the icy city, his breath vaporising. "I never said it," he began awkwardly, "but…thank you."

I raised my eyebrows, knowing it must be hard for him to accept help from others. After so long of being ostracised for being different, he'd expected me to leave him behind. Wilder had to get over it and realise that somebody actually cared about him—weird demon eyes, surly attitude, and all.

"I can see the wheels turning in that head of yours, Purples."

I grunted. "The metaphoric cogs are grinding."

"What are you thinking about?"

There was no one place to begin that made any sense. We were fighting for what we believed in, but Wainthrope believed he was too, and Markzoth. Their versions of right were twisted, but to them, so were ours.

"You can't have light without the dark," I said, watching the city. "There are shadows everywhere. Literal and metaphoric. No one is inherently good, just as no one is inherently bad."

Wilder nodded. "We can work together to make the world safe for us all. Naturals, humans—"

"Do you think the demons would ever settle for peace?"

He snorted. "History says no. There are things we can't let go, Purples. Demons are a parasitic species with a single purpose—to consume and destroy. There isn't any room for anyone else. With the one exception, of course…"

"Don't tell me you actually like Jackson now," I asked, shocked at his one-eighty.

"I gave the troll doll to Greer," he said, performing his favourite evasive manoeuvre. "It had all the information from that lab you blew up, and all the names of the humans with suspected mutations."

I knew Greer would spearhead the group that would search for them. They'd bring them back to the Sanctum, and Ramona would do her best to stop the mutations from spreading…if it wasn't already too late. Now that Markzoth was gone, we had a real chance at stopping Human Convergence for good.

"You have this annoying habit of changing the subject when you don't want to talk about something," I said, "it's blatant and annoying."

"Technically you're still a trainee, Purples. You better watch out, otherwise I'll request for your probation to be reinstated."

I opened my mouth to complain, but he was grinning. For that, he earned himself a slap on the arm, but he should be thankful I didn't push him off the roof.

I thought about Jackson then, and the promise I made him.

Wilder rolled his eyes. "What now?"

"I'm thinking about the druidess."

"Don't burst all your brain cells. She'll never give up any of her secrets."

I grunted. "Why did she meet with us? I get the feeling this was all part of some cosmic conspiracy."

"The druidess allowed us to meet with her because we were different," he explained. "She was different from her kind, too."

I wondered if that's why she'd lived for so long. Concealing herself in a city rife with supernatural war was dangerous, but also genius.

"Do you think she's good or bad?" I wondered out loud.

"I think she's in a league of her own."

"She knew it was a trap," I stated. "She knew what we were walking into and didn't say a thing."

"I'm sure she had her reasons."

I shook my head. It was useless to try to unravel the mystery of that woman. "You were right about her."

"I'm always right," he quipped.

"I have to get Jackson back," I added. "He could help Ramona with the others."

"And you made a promise."

"You heard that?"

"I didn't have too." He raised his eyebrows. "You kissed him at the safehouse."

"It's not like that between us," I said, watching him closely. Why would he bring that up? "We're family. We look out for one another."

He didn't even flinch. "I know."

Squashing down my disappointment, I looked out over the city towards Covent Garden.

"When you killed the Balan, you avenged your parents." He said it as if the moment should've given me closure, but revenge didn't bring back what was lost. I still didn't know who they were, let alone where I'd come from.

My worries must've translated to my face because Wilder slid his arm around me and pulled me close.

"You know who you are now," he murmured. "If that's all you know, then——"

"It's not enough." I lay my head on his shoulder, the unfamiliar embrace feeling like the most natural thing in the entire world. "I don't even understand what I did. That power…"

"Scarlett," Wilder sighed, his breath tickling the top of my head, "you weren't just touched by Arondight. A part of it lives inside you."

It was the only explanation that made sense. The way I used my Light, how the Codex called to me, how my Light spoke to Wilder's, how I was able to heal Jackson and myself, and how I was able to kill a greater demon… I could do things I wasn't supposed to.

I ran my fingers over my scar, the burden on my shoulders feeling heavier. Without me, Arondight would never resurface.

"I made a promise," I said, peeling myself away from Wilder's warmth. "I have to go tonight while the demons are still running scared."

"Do you want me to come with you?"

"I think we've established that I can do the solo thing and not get skewered anymore."

He smirked. "Don't let all that power go to your head, Purples."

"Any tips, boss?" I teased.

"She's a druidess, not human."

"I know. Her body is a vessel for something else."

Wilder looked impressed. "You've been studying."

"It wasn't easy. There wasn't much in the library *or* the Codex. The Druids are meant to have died out a long time ago, and they were annoyingly cryptic back then, too."

"So I hear."

"This about me and her," I said, staring out at the London skyline. "The things she said…" I shook my head.

Wilder nudged me with his elbow. "Your first solo mission. They grow up so fast…"

"*Smart-arse.*"

He grinned and nodded towards the city. "Go kick her arse, Purples."

## 21

S even Dials was shrouded in thick fog.

Darkness permeated every inch of the twisted crossroads, the red- and silver-tinselled Christmas decorations hanging across shop fronts and street lamps, shimmering through the mist. Snow was piled up on either side of the road, turning brown and mushy in the gutters.

My hands were thrust deep into my pockets as I walked down the alley, making my way towards the inner courtyard of shops and cafés known as Neal's Yard. Fairy lights twinkled overhead as I pushed aside the illusion guarding the druidess's hideout.

The narrow house was as we'd left it, squashed between the vegan bakery and the organic skincare shop, hidden by an intricate veil of magic. It wasn't Light and nothing at all like Darkness. It was an intricate kaleidoscope of something far older than anything either side of the war wielded.

Impatient, I shoved the door open and strode into

the living room, swatting a dangling strand of ivy out of the way.

I was surprised to find Jackson sitting on the couch with the druidess…*drinking tea*. There were no creepy rituals underway, or torture, or experimentation with those Darkness-infested runes. There was just a pot of English Breakfast and a pair of cups and saucers—and a feeling like they were waiting for me.

"Scarlett." Jackson rose to his feet and glanced at the druidess.

She stared at me, her eyes shining like a rainbow after a rainstorm and sipped her tea.

"I made a promise," I said to her, "and I intend to keep it."

Setting down her cup and saucer, she shook her head and patted Jackson on the knee. "I knew you'd do it."

I glanced at Jackson and he shrugged.

"The Balan demon is dead," I confirmed. "We found the lair and its name was useless."

"Not useless," she said, scowling. "Barrier."

"I'm sick of your riddles. You knew it was a trap. Why did you trick us?"

"I can tell you things," she said, ignoring my question. Wilder warned me, but I'd foolishly hoped she'd give a straight answer for once. "I saw you as a child. Little more than a baby. Violet, lavender, indigo. You poor child, always surrounded by blood and death. Blood and death… Thrust into the world alone. Lost. Always lost…"

I hesitated. "Did you know my parents?"

"I knew I couldn't avoid it," she muttered. "I knew, but I can try anyway. Try to change it. The future is unwritten, but the past holds all the secrets. All the power. Past losses, reborn futures…"

"Is she speaking in tongues?" Jackson asked, tilting his head to the side. "I can't understand a single thing she's saying."

The druidess rose from the couch and shuffled towards me. "It's time. I waited. *Take*." She smiled and opened her arms. "I'm tired. *Take*."

It took me a full minute to realise she was asking me to end her life. "I can't do that. No, I—"

"I saw. I knew. Always."

"You foresaw your death?" I whispered. *She'd seen me kill her.*

"A long time ago."

That meant I had no say in what was happening to me. I didn't like it. Only I had control over my future, but was it just an illusion? All of this—the runes, keeping Jackson hostage, helping Markzoth lure me into his lair—it was all designed to get me to come back here on my own, yet another manipulation.

"Family," she said, pressing something small and hard into my hand. "Keep."

"What?" My voice was soft as I closed my fingers around the unknown gift. "I don't understand. I—" I sensed the Darkness rising out of the runes and into the druidess, and I cried out, "*Stop!*"

But it was too late. The energy she'd unleashed

rushed towards me at an alarming speed and I threw up my hands. My Light shone before me, reflecting the attack with ease. It bounced into the wall, shattering off a woody arm of wisteria.

The druidess cried out in glee and clapped her hands together.

"Jackson, get behind me," I snarled, glaring at the druidess. He scurried across the room, putting distance between him and his captor.

The druidess held up her hands again and called on the runes. There were no words or incantations, but I felt it all around her. *Intent.*

"Don't make me do it," I pleaded. "You're the last of your kind. We could learn so much from each other. Don't waste your life."

"It is already done," she replied. "Strike, purple girl."

Power rushed for me once more and I deflected it, tears welling in my eyes. The blow glanced off my forearms and slammed into the old woman. She fell onto the floor in a heap, her shimmering eyes staring at the wisteria hanging from the ceiling.

Standing over her, I unsheathed my arondight blade. Violet sparks lit up the tangle of greenery, making the house glow as if the plants had taken a radioactive turn for the worse.

"*It's you.*" Her eyes widened and a strange smile pulled at her lips. "So beautiful..."

A white plume of smoke poured out of her mouth and billowed into the air. I didn't have the heart to thrust my blade through her essence, but I didn't have to. The while plume dissipated, hovering in the centre of the room like a heavy fog on a hard winter's morning.

Then…

She was gone.

Jackson peered over my shoulder, his eyes wide. "Was she—"

"No," I said. "She was a druidess, remember? They live a long time."

"She's dead, then?"

I nodded. "It was her choice. Her time."

Looking down at my palm, I found a small silver coin. What the druidess thought I could do with that, I didn't know. There were strange symbols cast into the metal that meant nothing to me. Slipping it into my pocket, I sheathed my arondight blade and gave the druidess one last look.

"Let's get out of here," I said after a moment.

Outside, the air shimmered. The fog had thickened, reflecting a rainbow of colours—the druidess's parting gift to Seven Dials.

"Do you think she really knew your parents?" Jackson asked as we made our way across the courtyard.

"Lies," I replied, the coin heavy in my pocket. "They were all lies."

"Are you sure?"

I grunted, not wanting to talk about it. "Did she hurt you?"

He shook his head. "She made me drink tea."

"Tea? Not some herbal concoction? That stuff can hold some real power, Jackson."

"Na." He shrugged. "It was Twinings English Breakfast."

Wilder was right about her just being a lonely old woman, which made me feel worse about ending her life. It was what she wanted, though, and she'd gone to a lot of trouble to orchestrate it, but it wasn't comforting. I just wanted Jackson to have the freedom he deserved.

"Where to now?"

"The Sanctum," I replied. "Greer has rolled out the welcome wagon for you, but—"

"She doesn't know about..." He nodded towards the druidess's house.

"No. And I think we'd better leave it that way." The shadows were creeping back in now that the druidess's magic had vanished.

"Cool. Times are tough. I get it." A rumble echoed through the courtyard and Jackson frowned. "What now?"

I knew before I even looked. "The house."

We turned and watched as the narrow building groaned and shook. The skincare shop and the vegan bakery pressed in from either side, squashing the ramshackle cottage with immense force, cracking and splintering the wooden frame. Finally, the two shop fronts collided with a dull boom. The sound echoed through my bones as we watched the city swallow the last of the druidess's home whole.

When it was gone, I turned, walking towards

Seven Dials. I shoved my hands into my pockets, the coin pressed firmly in my clenched fist.

It was time to take another path, one that would hopefully lead to my parents and ultimately, Arondight.

*Seven obscure passages. Seven different roads. A place for the less fortunate to find their fate.*

---

**Scarlett's adventure continues with DARK ABANDON, the third book in the thrilling Arondight Codex!**

*A high school do-over.*
*A plot to take out a whole generation of Naturals.*
*And Scarlett Ravenwood is in the thick of it… again.*

# ABOUT NICOLE

**Nicole R. Taylor** is an Australian Urban Fantasy author.

She lives in the western suburbs of Melbourne dreaming up nail biting stories featuring sassy witches, duplicitous vampires, hunky shapeshifters, and devious monsters.

She likes chocolate, cat memes, and video games.

When she's not writing, she likes to think of what she's writing next.

### Follow Nicole Online:

*Website*: www.nicolertaylorwrites.com
*Twitter*: twitter.com/nicole_noir
*Facebook:* facebook.com/nrtaylorwrites
*Newsletter:* www.nicolertaylorwrites.com/newsletter
**Email:** nicole.this.is@gmail.com

# DARK ABANDON (THE ARONDIGHT CODEX - BOOK THREE)

**A high school do-over.
A plot to take out a whole generation of Naturals.
And Scarlett Ravenwood is in the thick of it...** *again.*

Scarlett Ravenwood never though she'd end up in the centre of a supernatural apocalypse, least of all going back to *high school*.

After tapping into the drop of Arondight she holds inside her, she knows she's in over her head. Unable to control her Light, she's sent to the Academy where the next generation of Naturals are being trained, but something sinister is lurking underneath the surface. The headmaster believes one of the students is possessed... they just don't know who.

Going undercover, it's up to Scarlett and Wilder to root out the cause of the unrest and thwart the Dark's latest attempt at tipping the balance, before a whole generation is wiped out.

**With the next generation of Naturals in mortal danger, can Scarlett unravel the mystery surrounding her forgotten past in time to save them from the demon horde?**

*Find out in Dark Abandon, the third novel in The Arondight Codex, an Urban Fantasy series full of adventure, mystery, and romance, woven with the spirit of heroic Arthurian legend.*

------

**Dark Abandon, the third novel in The Arondight Codex, is out now!**